AN ABSOLUTELY SPLENDID ILLUSTRATED JOURNEY

BY

Michael W. Mosley

This book is dedicated to God, family, and friends.

In this book, there are many of my hand-drawn illustrations. Underneath each illustration, I have written a line or a couple lines to show what I thought about when I looked at the illustration on that page. The book is meant to be a source of entertainment for the viewer/reader.

Johnny Mack always could be seen around town toting an old worn guitar case. And most folks knew that he carried a nice old guitar in the case.

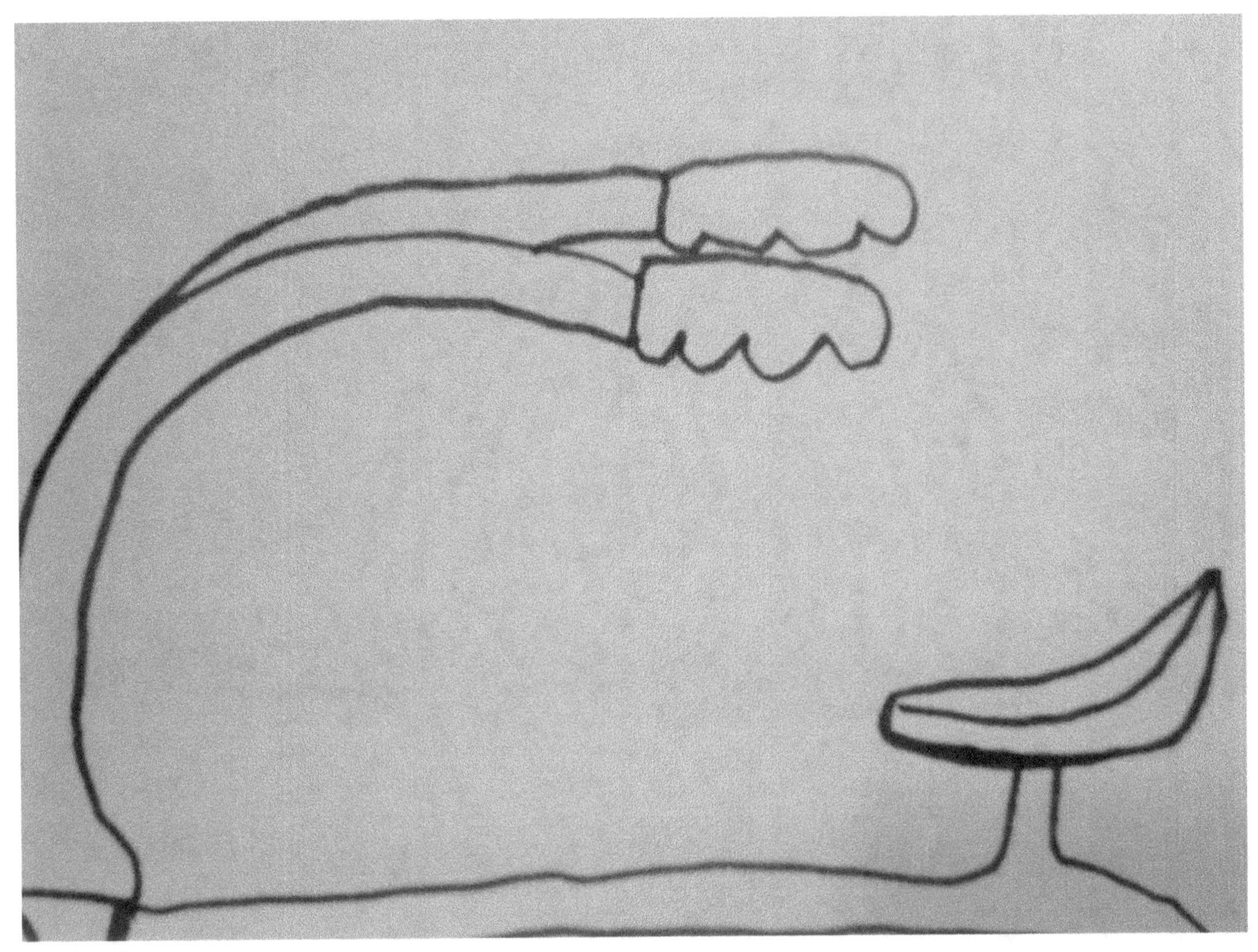

Tim Farrington liked to ride his bicycle approximately ten miles a day. He sometimes rode all the way to see his girlfriend, Janice, who lived in a town that was around sixteen miles away.

Benny Kraal bought himself a fine hat when he went into the thrift store. He told his buddies that it was the best deal that he ever got for a buck and a half.

Ted Tollack created a toothpaste that he called Bright Smiles. In less than five years, he became a millionaire from the sales of his creation.

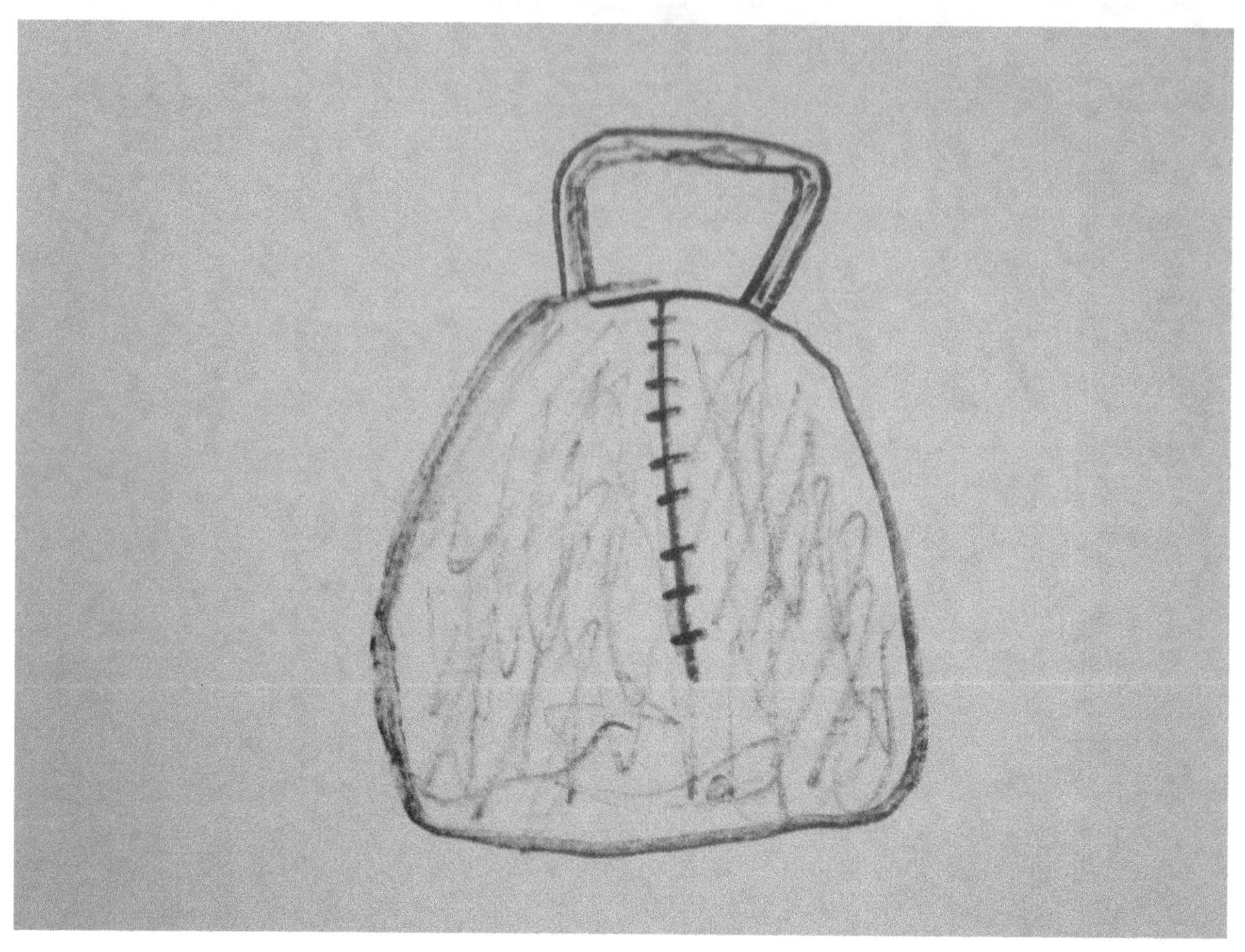

Riley Coogan kept all his money in an old bowling ball bag in the closet in his bedroom. He must have had over thirty thousand dollars in that old bag.

On Pontatock Hill, there stands an old oak tree that was the landmark for a buried treasure. No one would ever suspect that buried beside it, was a buried saddle bag filled with gold coins.

Henry Beckett built the old weathered bird house that hung from a limb in the back yard of his parent's home.

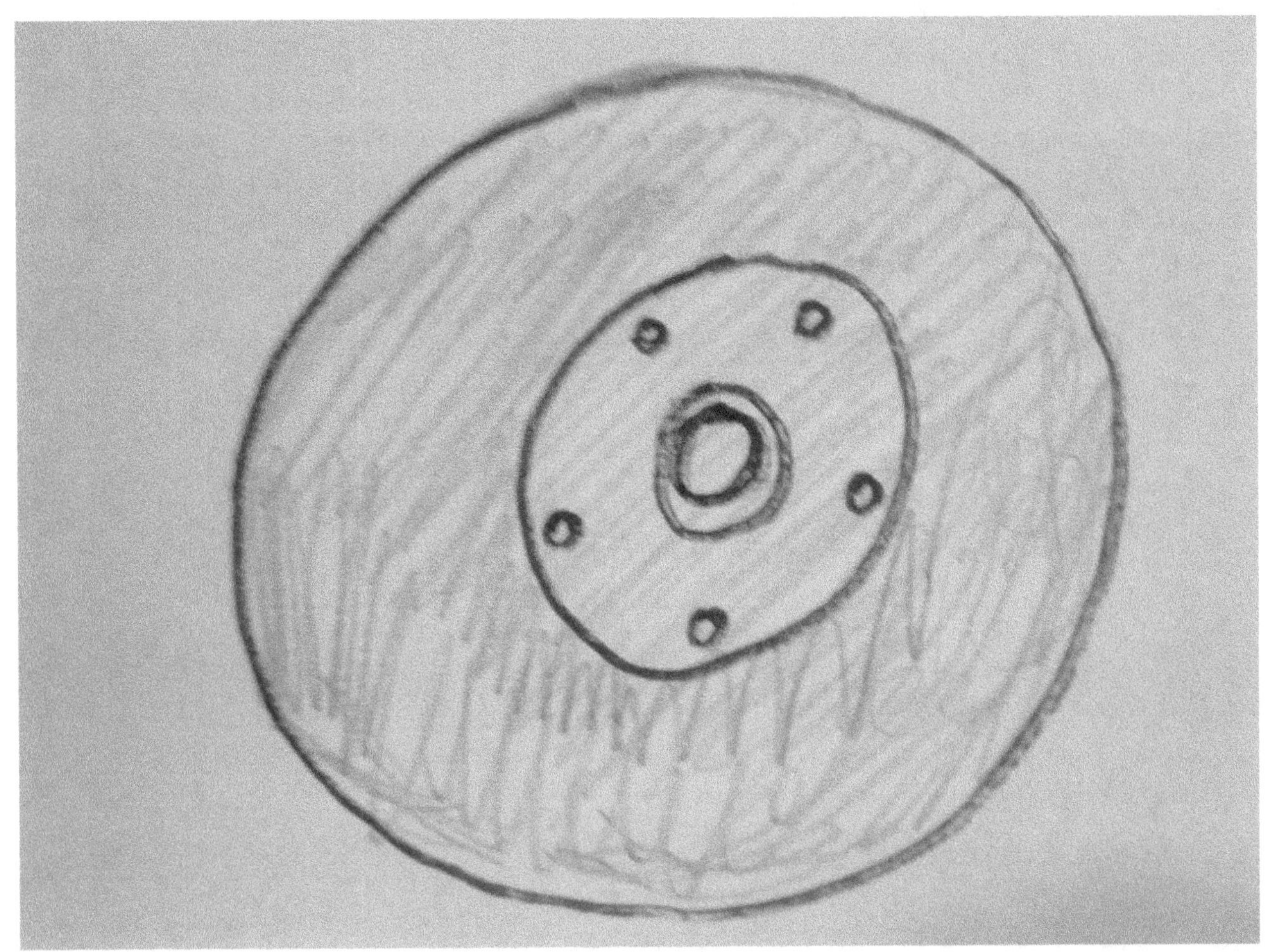

Will Diamond bought a good used tire from a service station five miles from his home. He was lucky that the service station owner had a tire that was the right size for his old car.

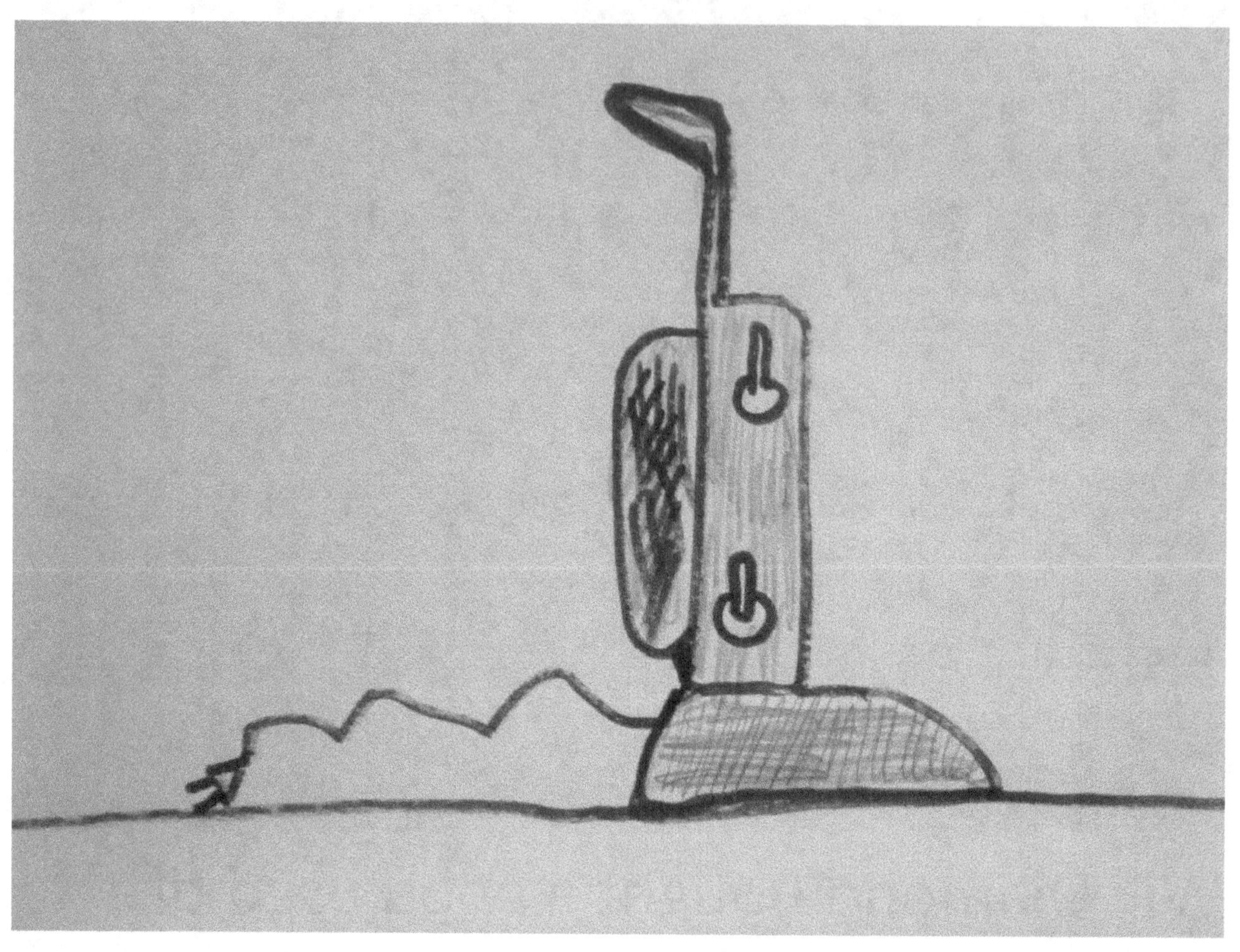

Suzie Brighton bought a new vacuum cleaner from a salesman who came knocking on her door. She thought that the vacuum cleaner was the best one that she ever had.

Sherrie Lynnville liked to keep exotic fish in her aquarium. She liked to watch the fish swim all around in the aquarium.

Bob Janks wasn't the best wood worker around. He built a wooden box that didn't end up being as good as he wanted it to be. He laughed and said, "I reckon it's good enough for government work." His buddy shrugged his shoulders and laughed.

Penny Slater's little dog would stand in the doghouse and look out. Penny would call it and it would come running just as fast as it could come.

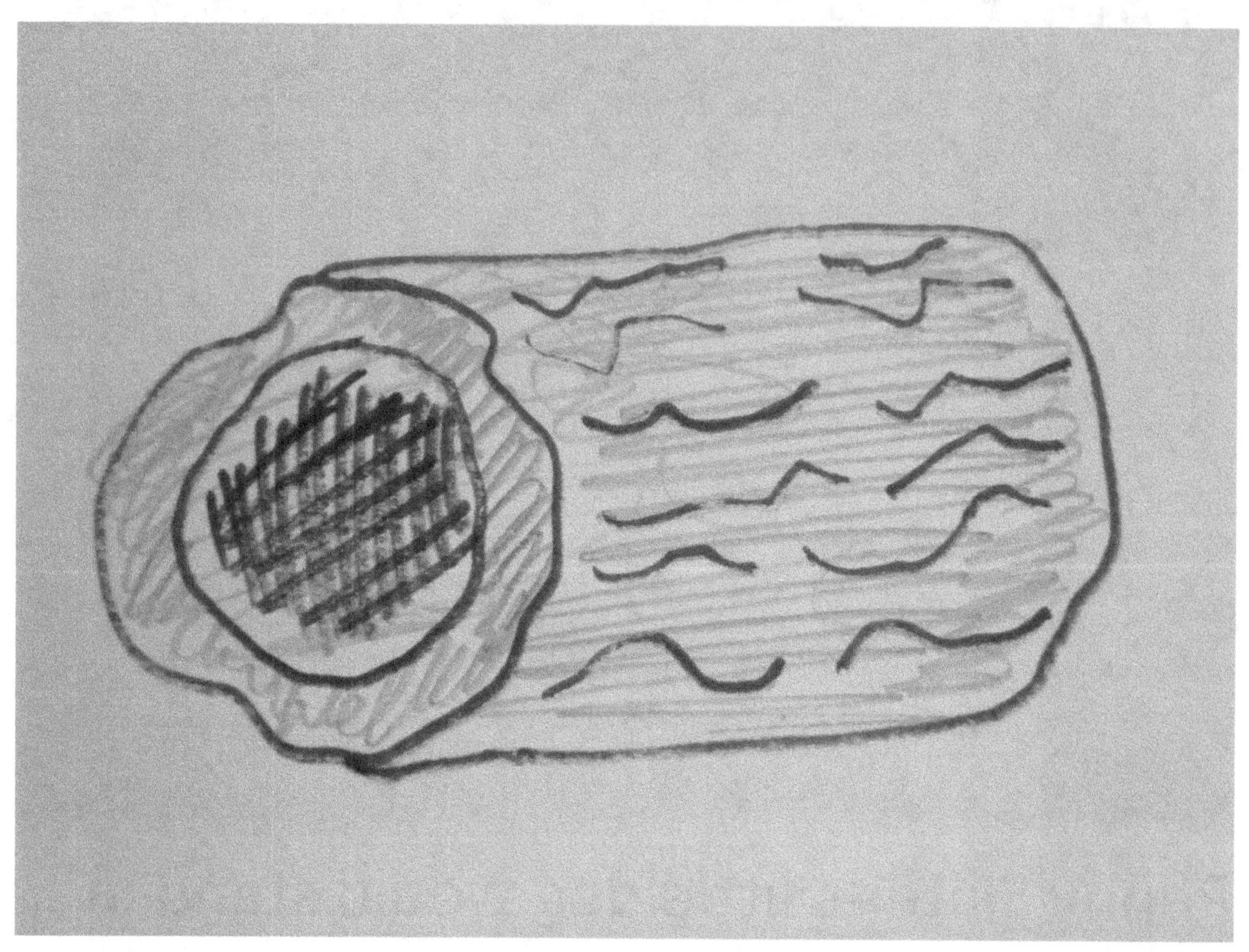

Jenny Parker saw a small animal run to a hollow log and hide inside. She wondered what the animal was, but she didn't bother the creature.

Johnny Ricter went into a local auto parts store and bought some wheel bearing grease. He had to replace the bearings in his old truck that he called "The mudhole buster".

Kelly Thornburg found an odd-looking rock in the middle of the road late one evening. When he showed it around to some friends, he found out that it was actually a meteorite.

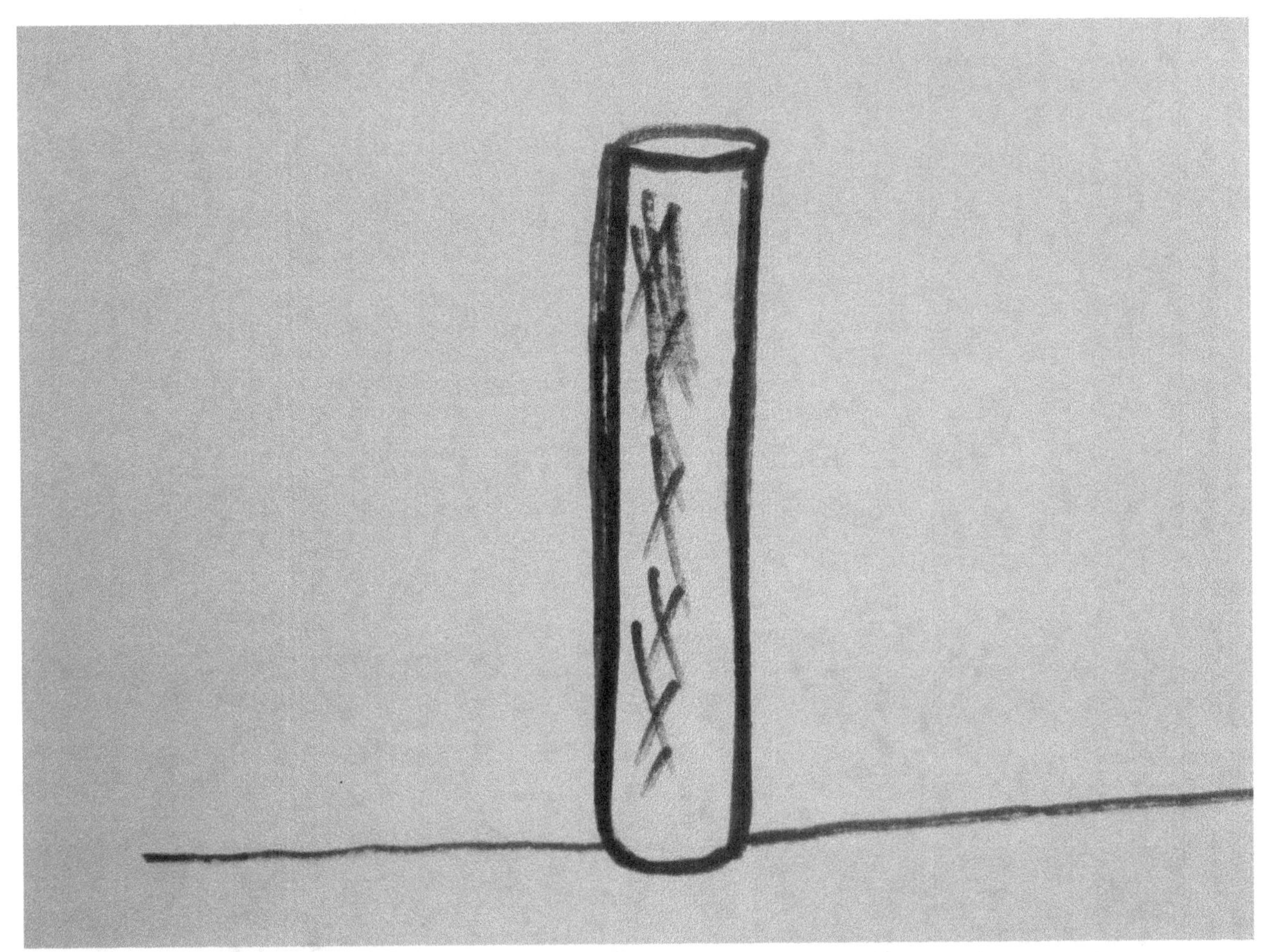

Johnny Langtree found an old piece of pipe with his metal detector. The pipe was sealed at both ends with wax. After he removed the wax from one end, he found out that the pipe was filled with silver dollars minted in the late 1800's.

Jack Larsen hid his money in the deep freezer by wrapping it with aluminum foil and labeling it LIVER. "Who would ever suspect that that package of

"LIVER" really was a package containing several thousand dollars?" he said to himself.

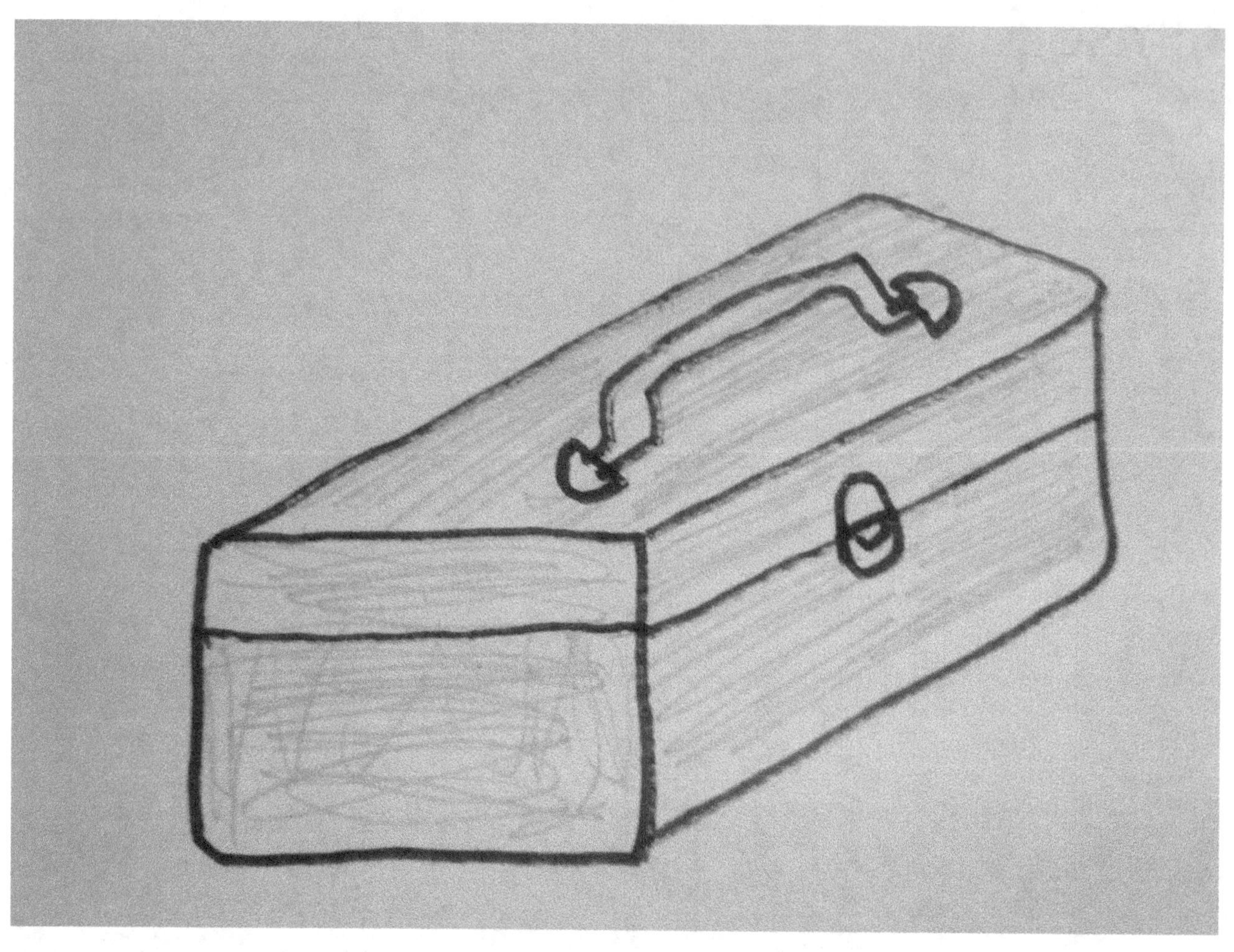

For 27 years, Willie Muldoon carried his red toolbox to work with him. He had worked on all kinds of vehicles over the years, and he was surely ready to retire when the time came for him to do so.

Russell White would carry a bar of soap with him when he went to the creek. He would lather up and dive into the cold clear water. He wasn't the best swimmer, but he was the cleanest person at the old swimming hole.

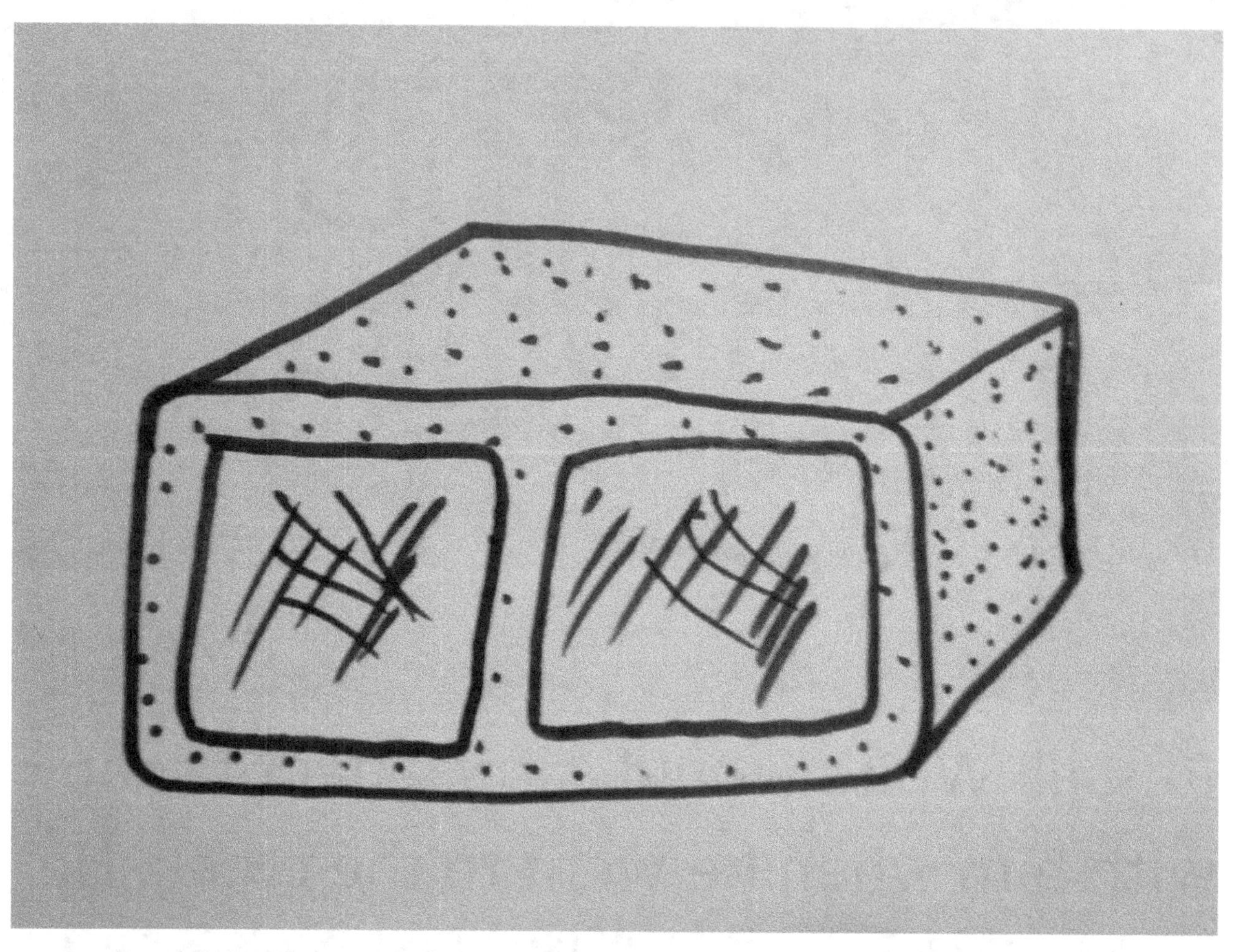

Billy Williams must have laid a million cement blocks in his days of working for The Greenway Construction Company. When he retired, he never laid another block again.

Morley Peat hid his money in an old paint bucket. He put the bucket on a shelf in his shed and no one ever suspected that that old can held a fortune.

Maddie Jackson loved the little Aloe Vera plant that her grandmother had given her. When she saw the plant, she thought of her grandmother.

Myron Johnson was just crazy about eating peanut butter. He ate it on toast. He ate it on apple slices. And he ate it all by itself.

Henry Wadsden liked to burn trash in an oil drum in the back yard of his home. He'd throw paper, sticks, and other things into the drum and set whatever was inside the drum on fire.

Ike Kay bought a new toilet after having to fix the old one for the sixth time.

Jack Minden used a metal detector to search around an old fireplace that stood in a field. He found a few silver coins and a few other artifacts in the ground.

Joe Whitmore liked to play with a Yo-Yo that his daddy had made for him. He could do tricks that impressed his friends. They would try to do some tricks themselves, but most of them weren't as good as he was at doing the tricks.

Little Jimmy Jones liked to watch the boats sailing by. He hoped to someday own a sailboat himself so that he could sail on the bay.

Bernie Crale drew a crude design on a sheet of paper, and told the tattoo artist, "I want one that says GOTTA HAVE LOVE"

Millie Crale decided that she wanted a tattoo that a star on it and had the words STAR SHINE on it.

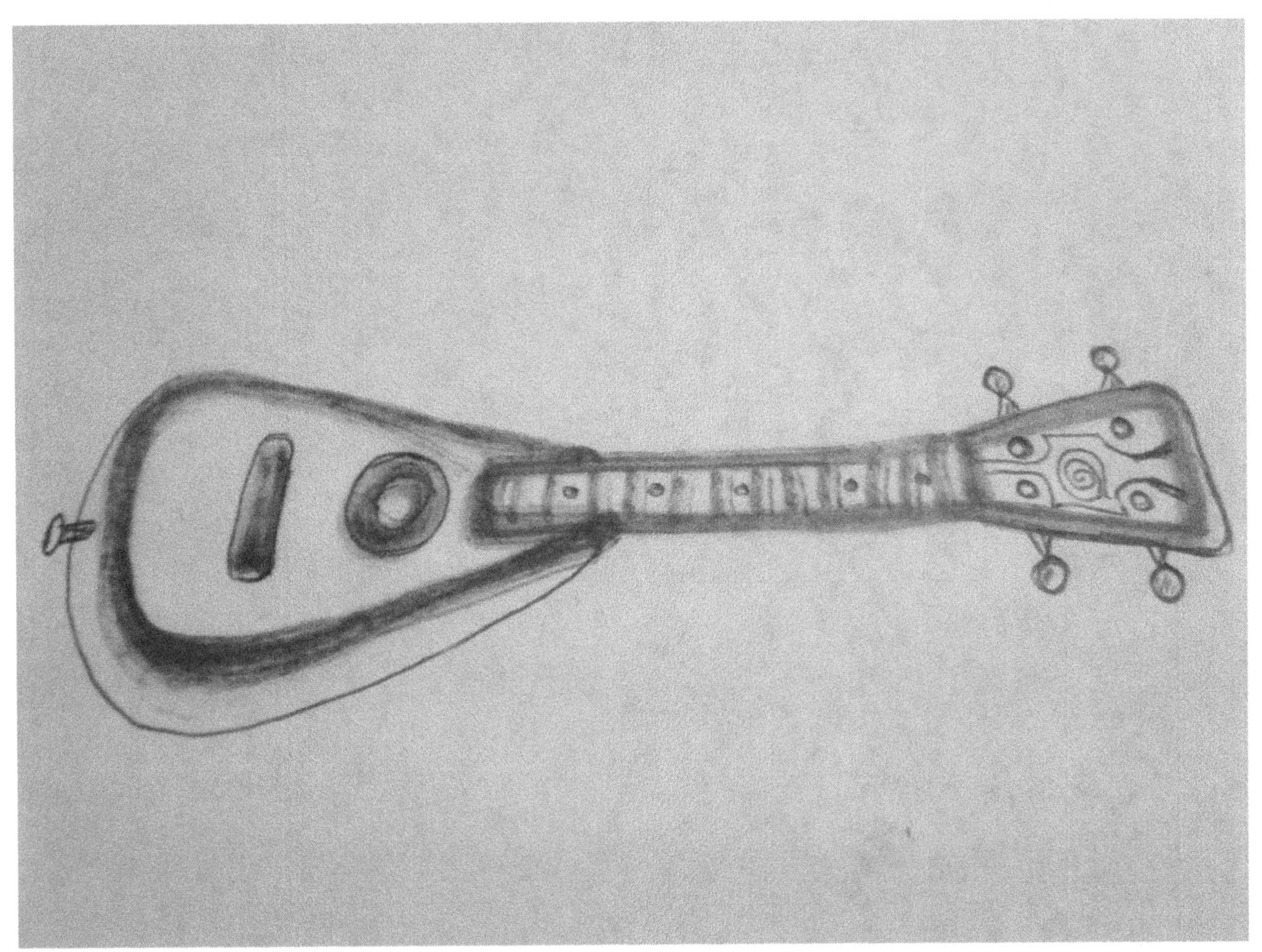

Willa Mae received a ukulele as a birthday gift from her mother. She read some books and taught herself how to play the instrument. Her friends and family enjoyed hearing her play.

Lena Winton and her boyfriend, Jack Warren, would meet at the old oak tree on Grider Hill and they'd talk up a storm while eating snacks and drinking cold soda. They enjoyed their meetings under the old tree.

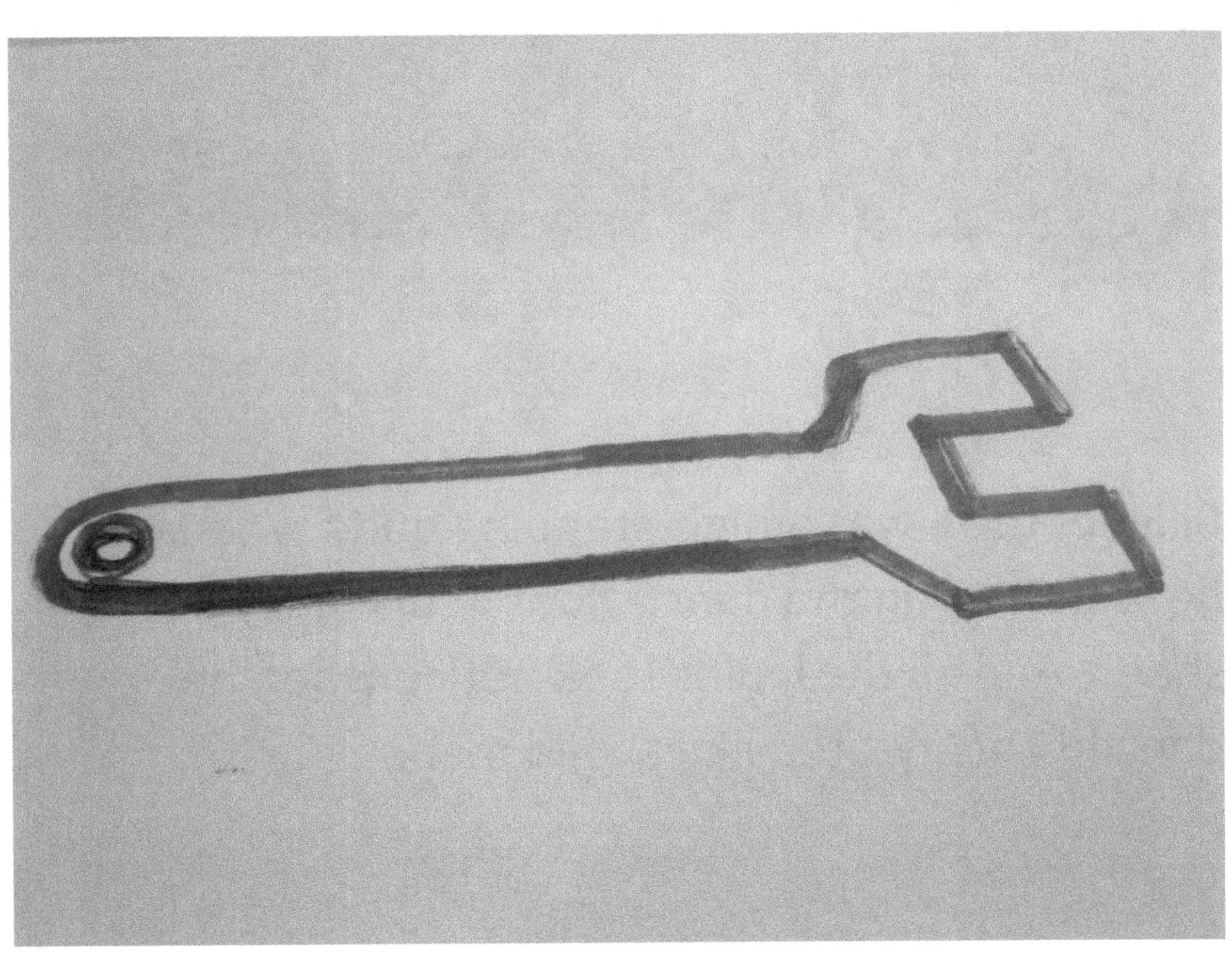

Jack Wint was always losing the wrench he used to work on his lawnmower. He decided to paint the wrench yellow so that he could see it better.

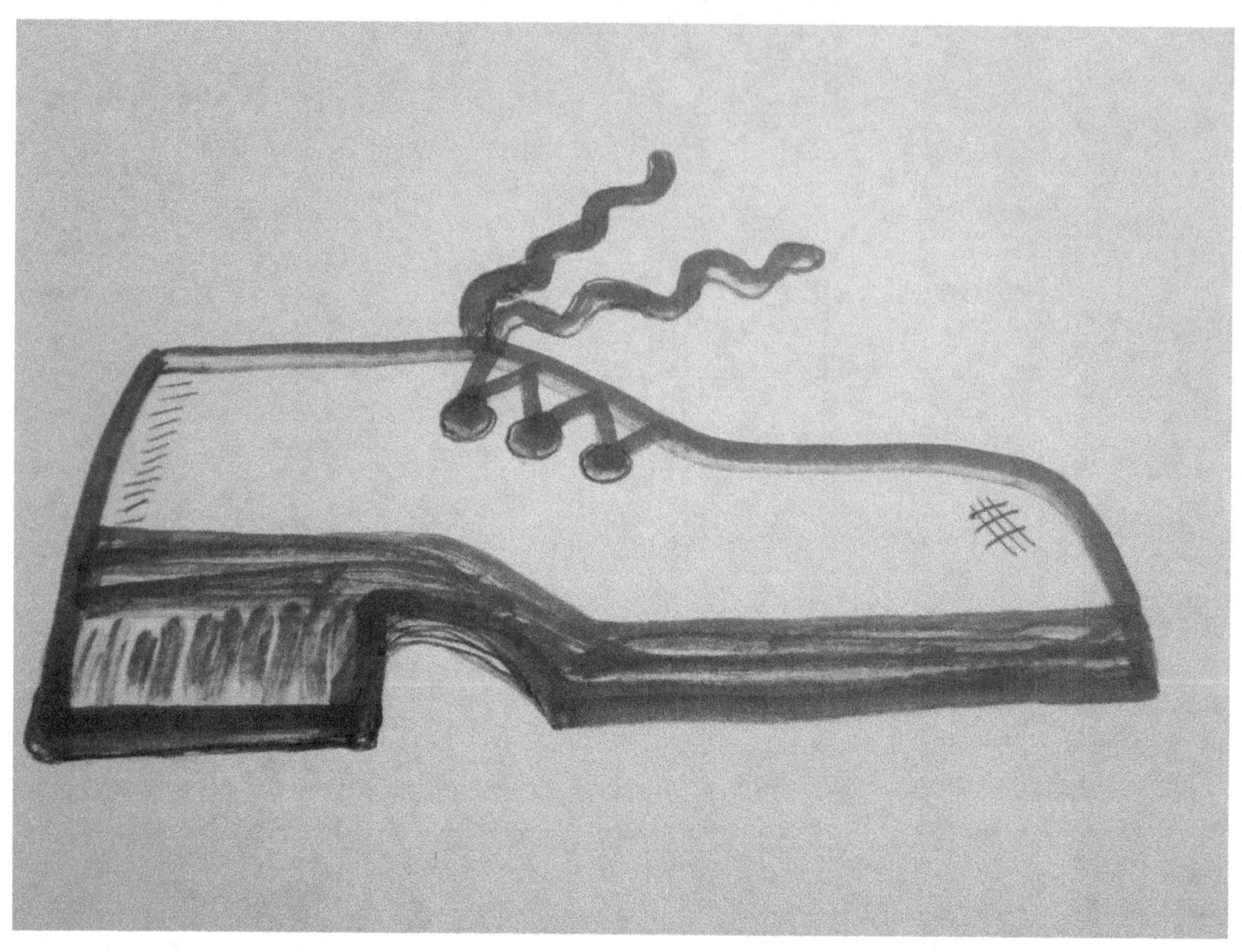

Billy Johnson was a high-stepping dude whenever he went out on the dance floor in his fancy new shoes. And all the ladies took notice when he danced and gyrated like a wild man.

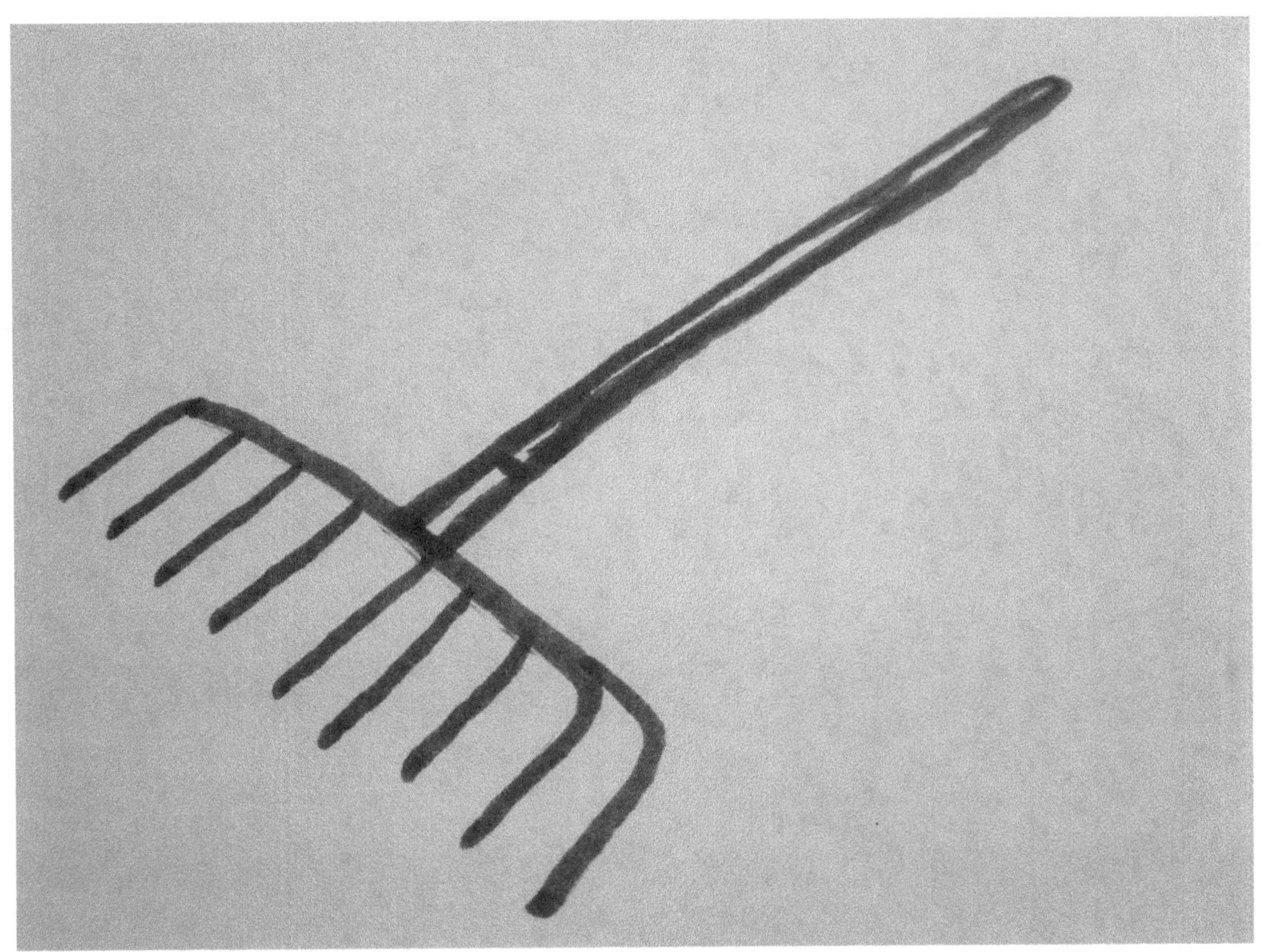

Jimmy Steffard raked his grandmother's yard so that he could earn enough money to take his girlfriend, Jessica, to a movie. They ate popcorn and slurped on sodas while a monster terrorized a town onscreen.

Jessica Brantner loved the old quilt that her grandmother had given her. The quilt was made from cloth pieces of many colors and shapes. It was priceless to her, and she would never part with it.

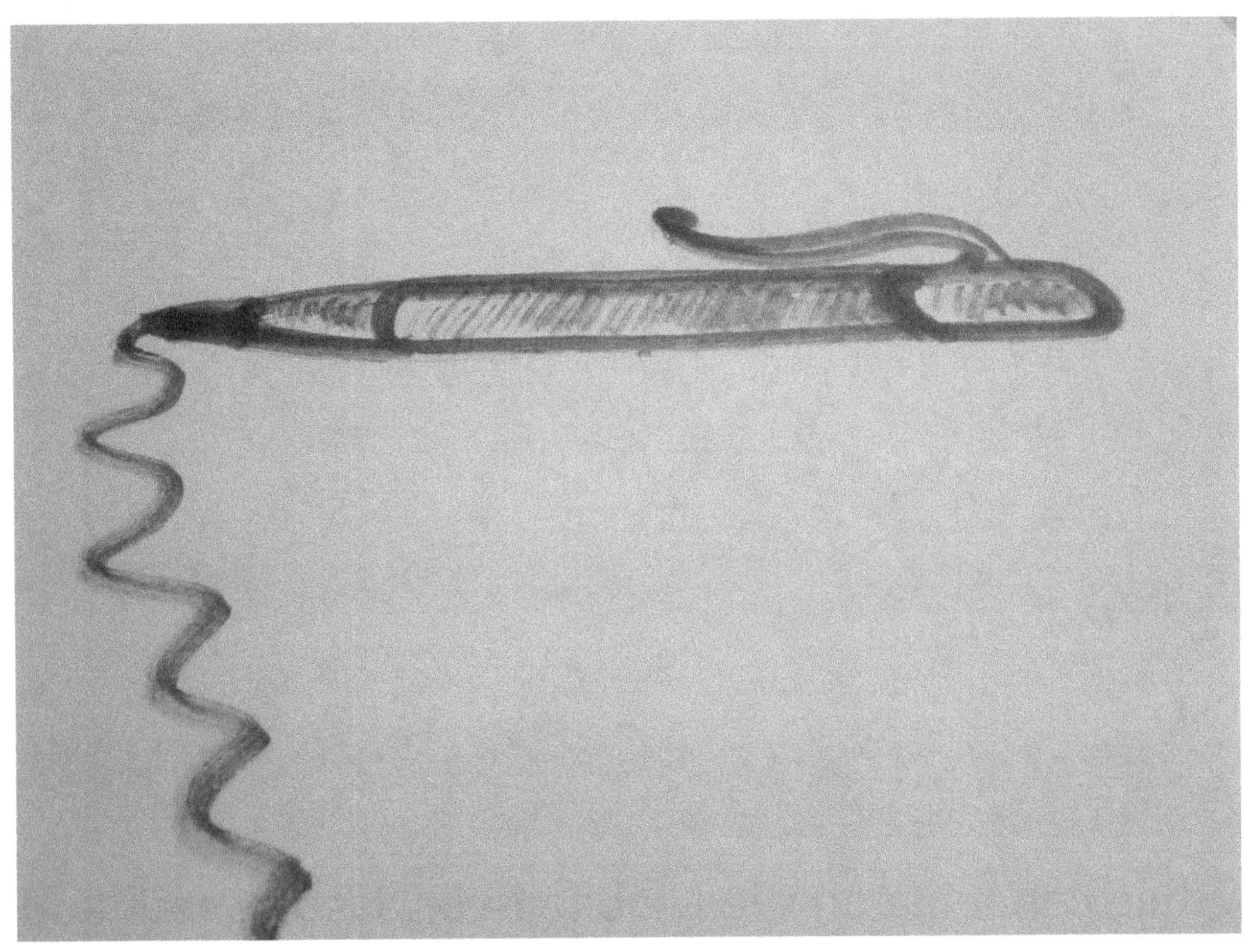

Kelly treasured the old pen that her mother had once owned. Her mother had used that pen to outline her first novel titled "THE REASONS WHY"

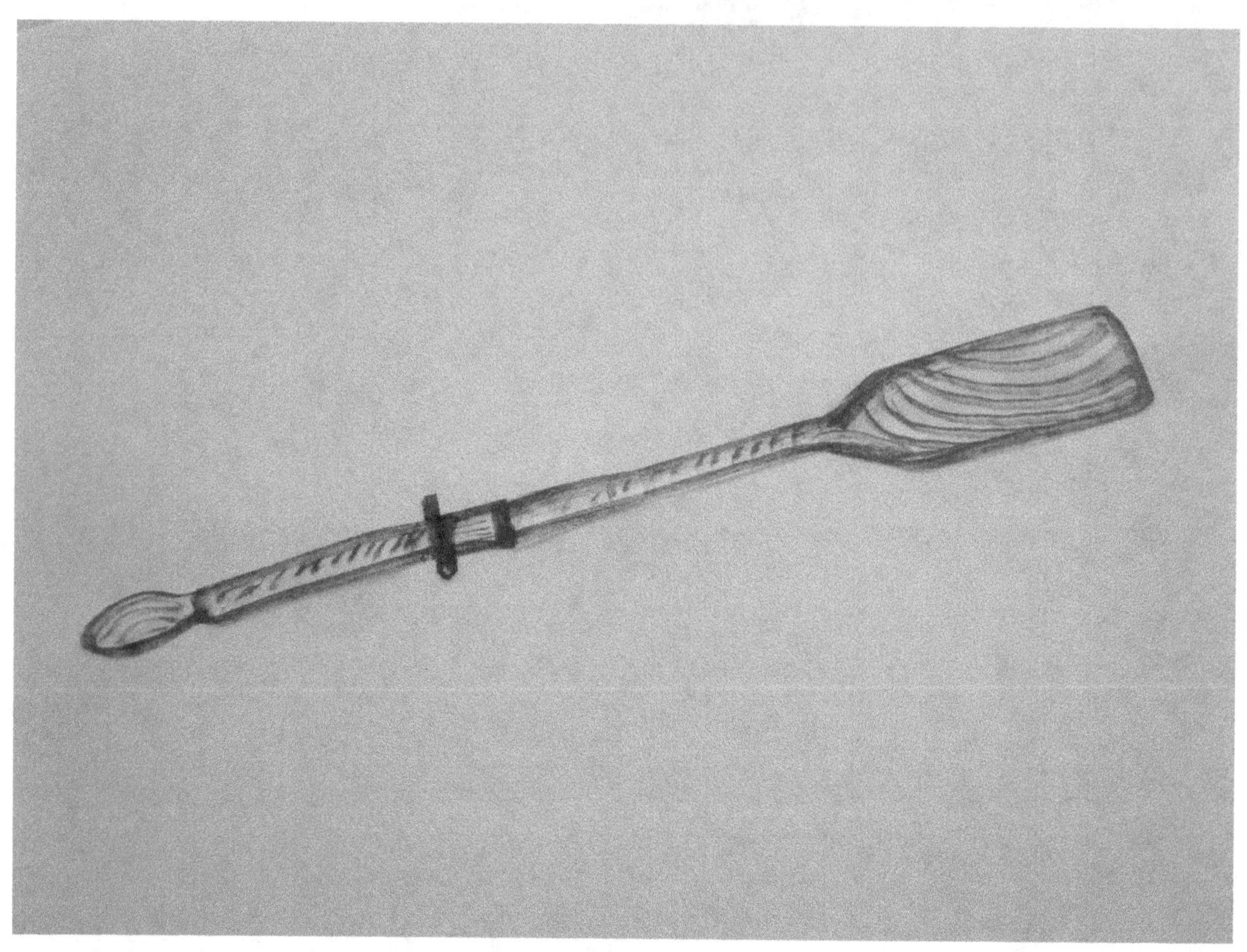

While canoeing on the Mobile river, Jason Lamb and his girlfriend, Shelly, found an old oar that someone had lost. And they wondered how they had lost the oar.

Some kind of vine was growing upwards toward the sky on Timmy Pollard's granfather's farm.Timmy looked closely at the vine, and thought about Jack And The Bean Stalk. He liked that old tale.

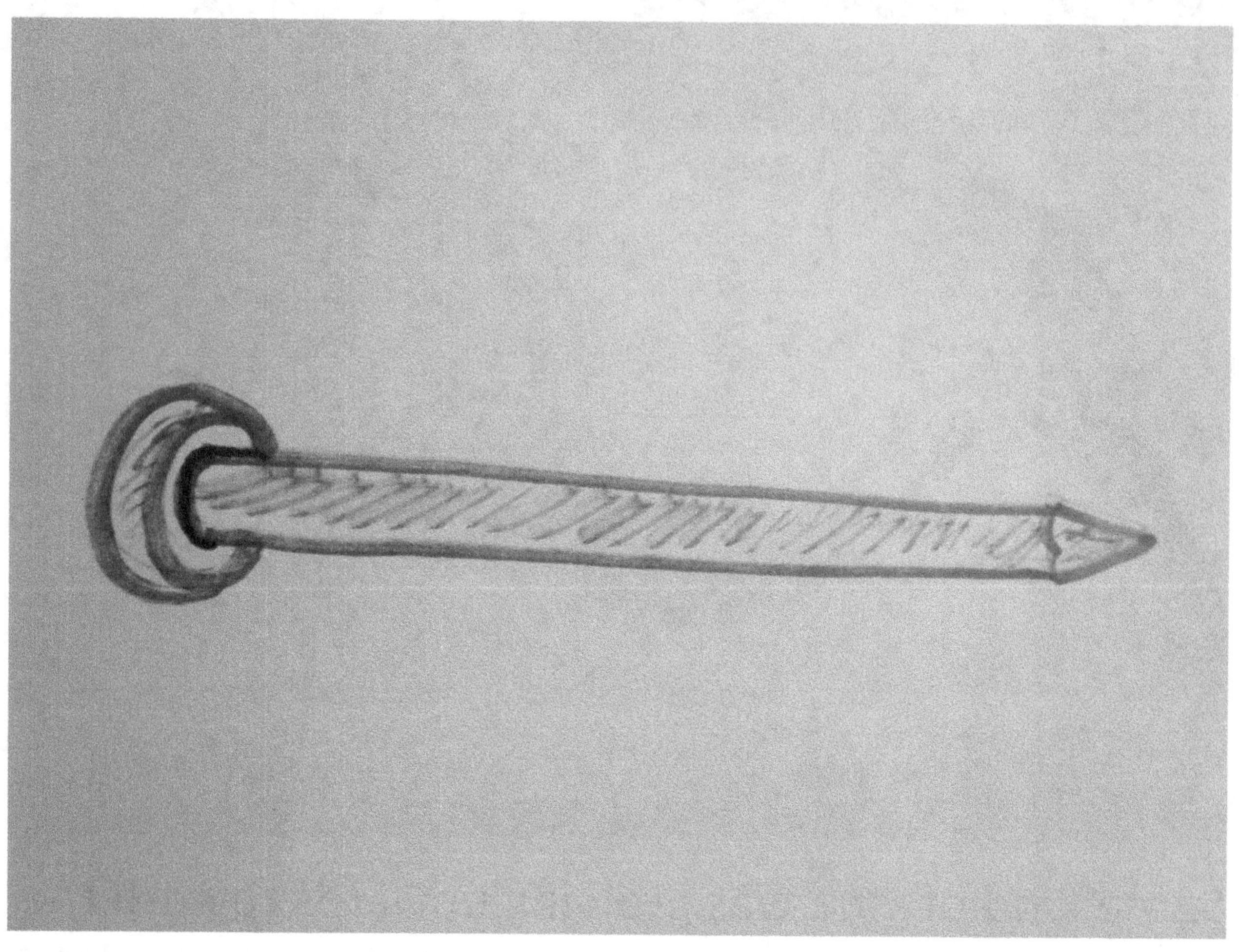

Westley Biggs looked at a large nail that sat on a shelf in his dad's shed, and he thought about the spikes that held Jesus Christ on the cross at Calvary.

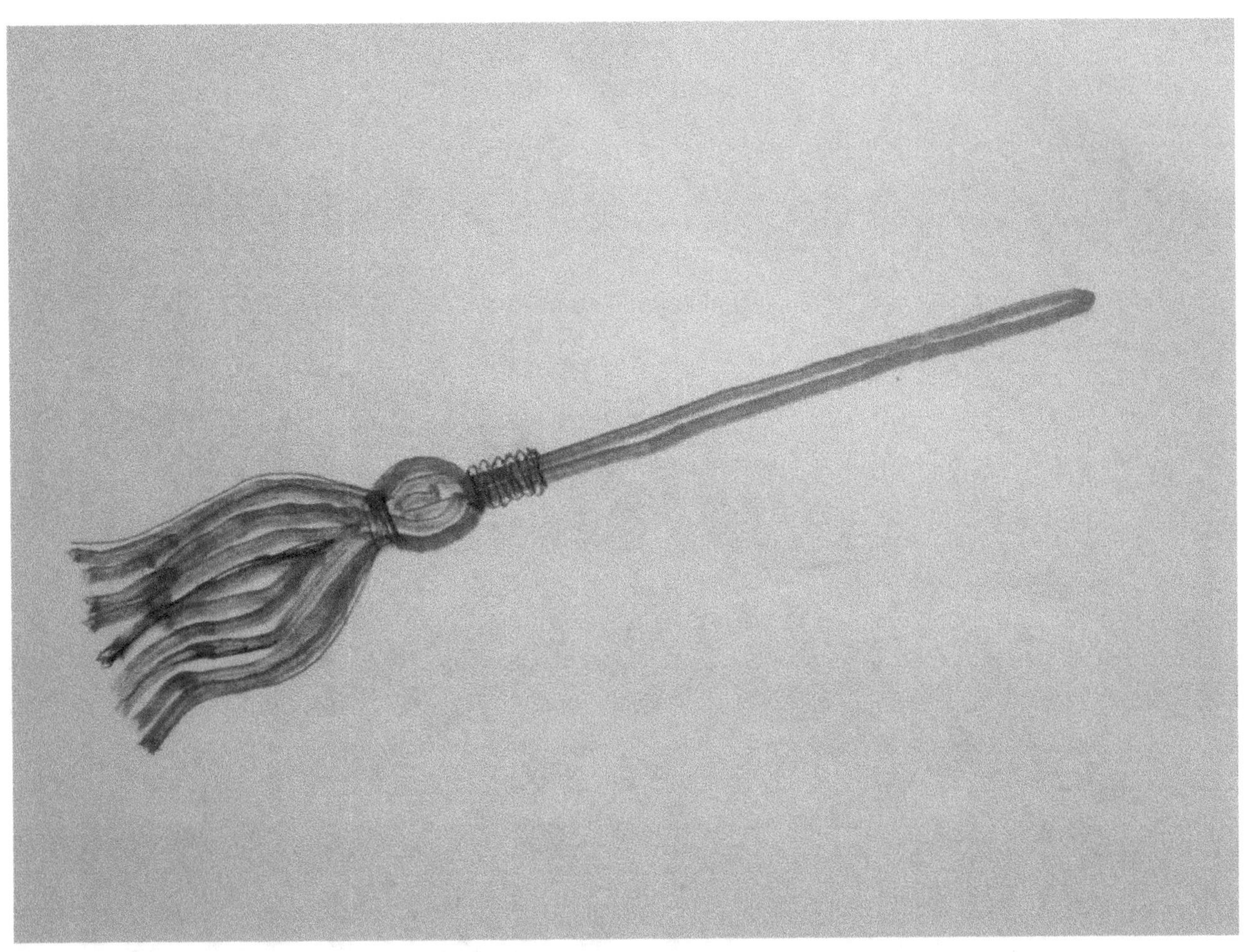

Jenny Culpepper's grandmother Florence used to sweep the floor of her house with a homemade broom. She'd say, "There's no store bought broom that's better than the ones I make."

Sandra West opened up a book and looked at a dried- out leaf that she had placed in the book many years previously. She found that leaf while on a date with her former boyfriend, Beau Bradly, back in 1956.

Tony Tarpin found a key on the ground near the picnic table where he and his girlfriend were eating. He figured that it was a key to one of the nearby beach houses.

Handley Johnson was a tough sort of guy. He didn't suffer smart alecks too lightly. On more than one occasion, he taught some fellow his lesson for being too smart with him.

James Conway looked at a small submarine that he saw sitting in the calm water of the bay. He wondered where the crew was at the moment. Eventually he saw a boat come u to the vessel and three men dove down and entered the submarine.

Kerry Stiles went into the local library every Saturday morning and he read the same book at the same table nearly every time that he went to the library. It was a curious thing to the library staff, but he didn't care what they thought. He was trying to learn a certain type of information.

A windmill once stood out in a field on Henry Ward's grandfather's farm. The windmill was finally torn down in the Summer of 1949.

Shelly Brant's grandmother used to use a pair of scissors to cut patterns out of the material that flour came in to make dresses for her two girls. The girls didn't feel ashamed of the dresses because other girls at school also wore dresses made from that type of cloth.

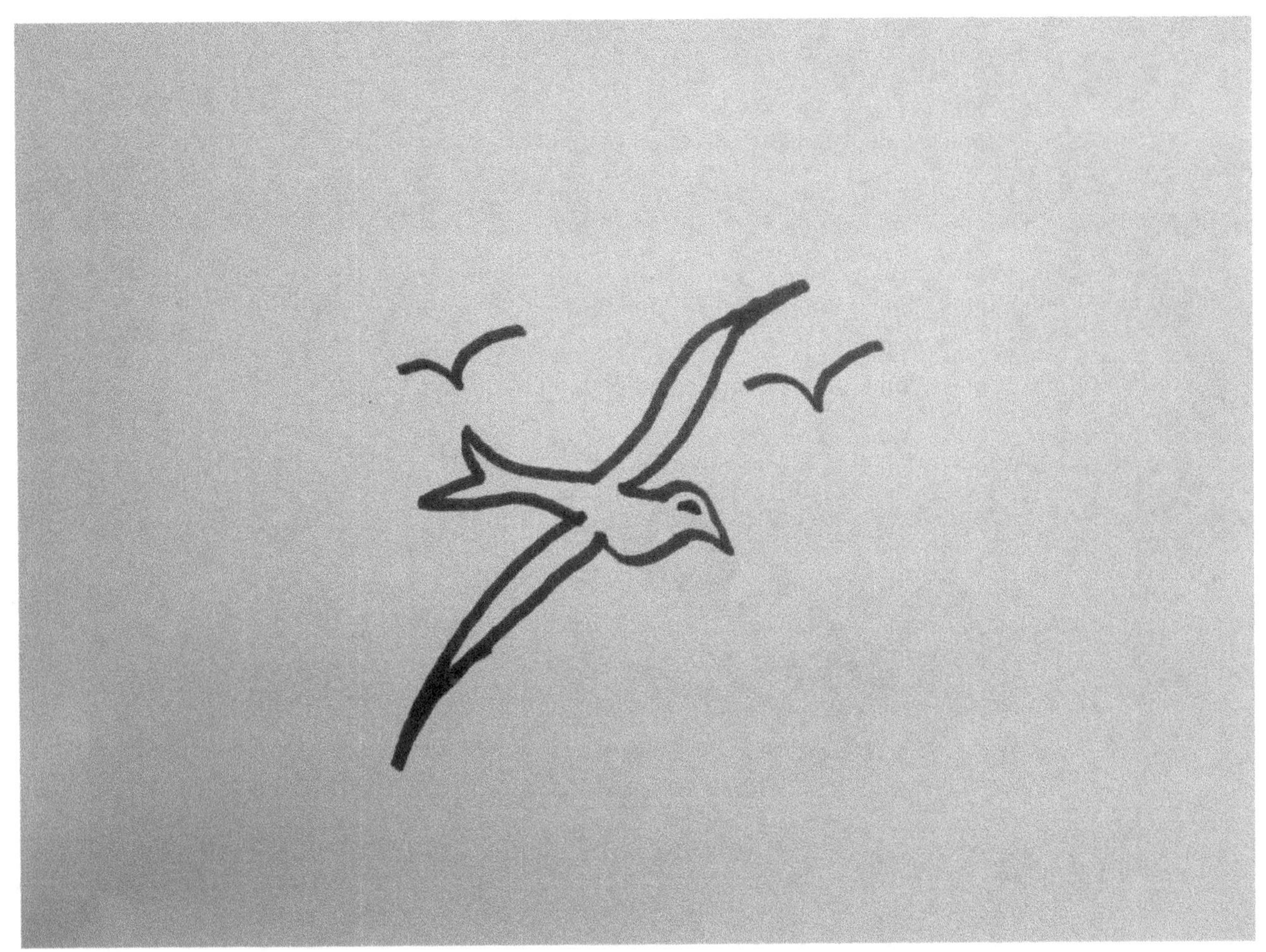

When Harriet and Sam Ogden went to the local beach, they liked to watch the seagulls gliding through the air above the waves.

Mark Warren owned a pen that had been used to write a novel by his great grandfather, Jeremiah Henson. Mark liked to hold the pen and think about writing a novel himself, but he never got around to doing so. He did write a few short stories, though.

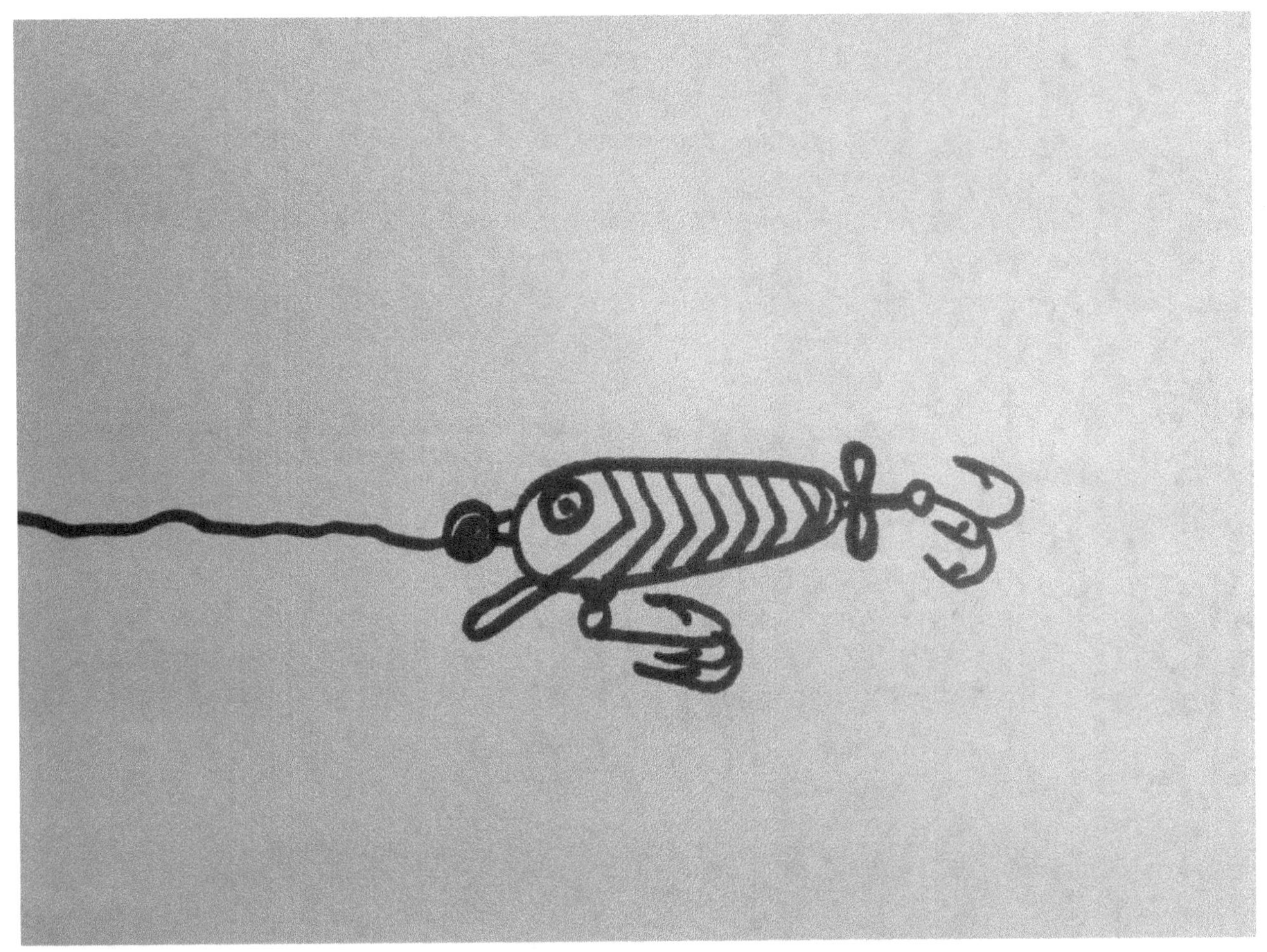

Tommy Smith's uncle, John Lee, used to have a favorite bass plug that he used to fish with. He caught many bass with that old plug. And he won some money in several local fishing tournaments.

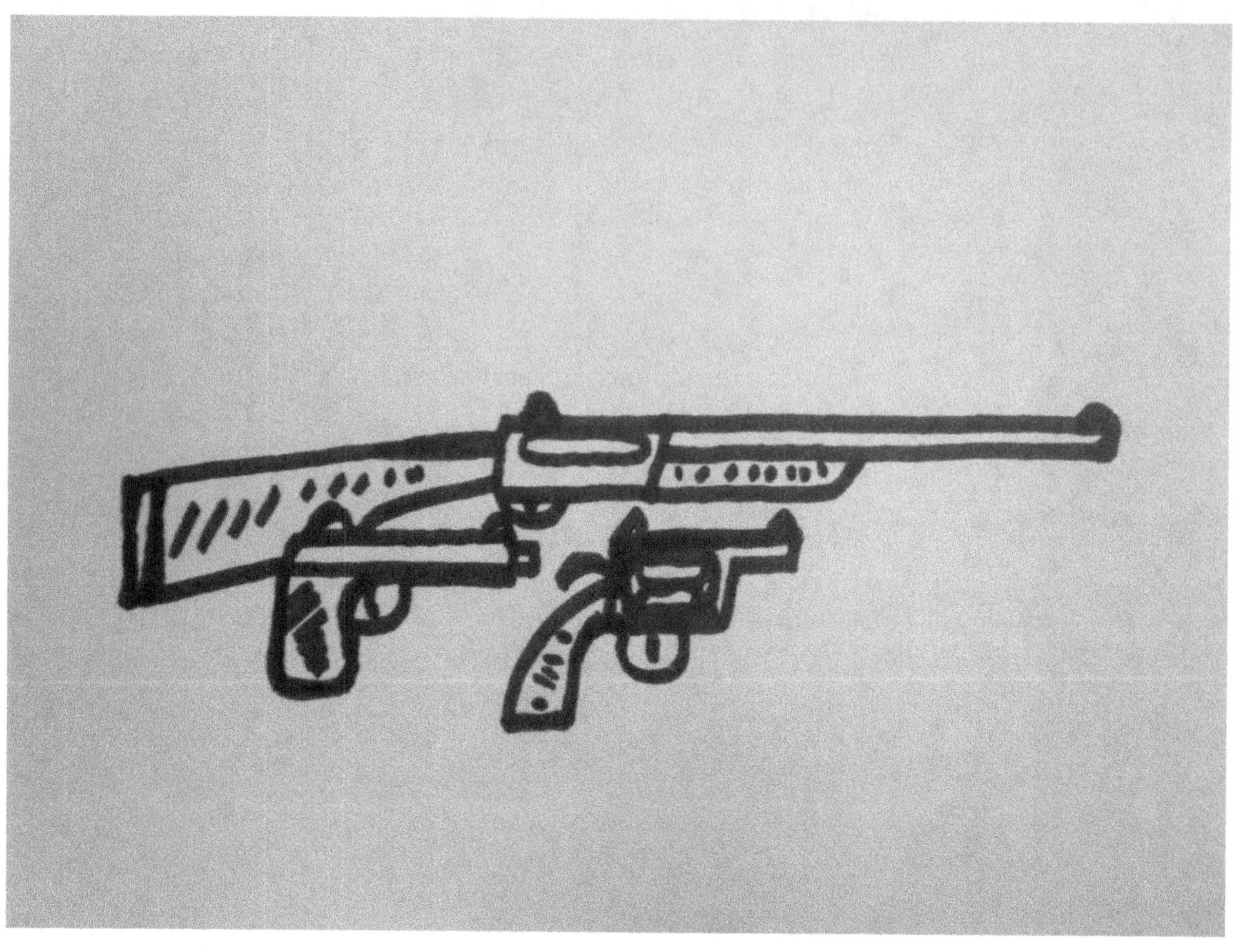

Matt Winton was a gun collector. He had many guns, and he liked to get out in his back yard and shoot them. His neighbors thought it sounded like a war broke out almost every Saturday afternoon.

Jenny Blake sat a pan on the counter and the smoke from the pan rose up in spirals. "God, that stuff smells good," her husband said. Jenny smiled and said, "It better, I've been cooking it for an hour."

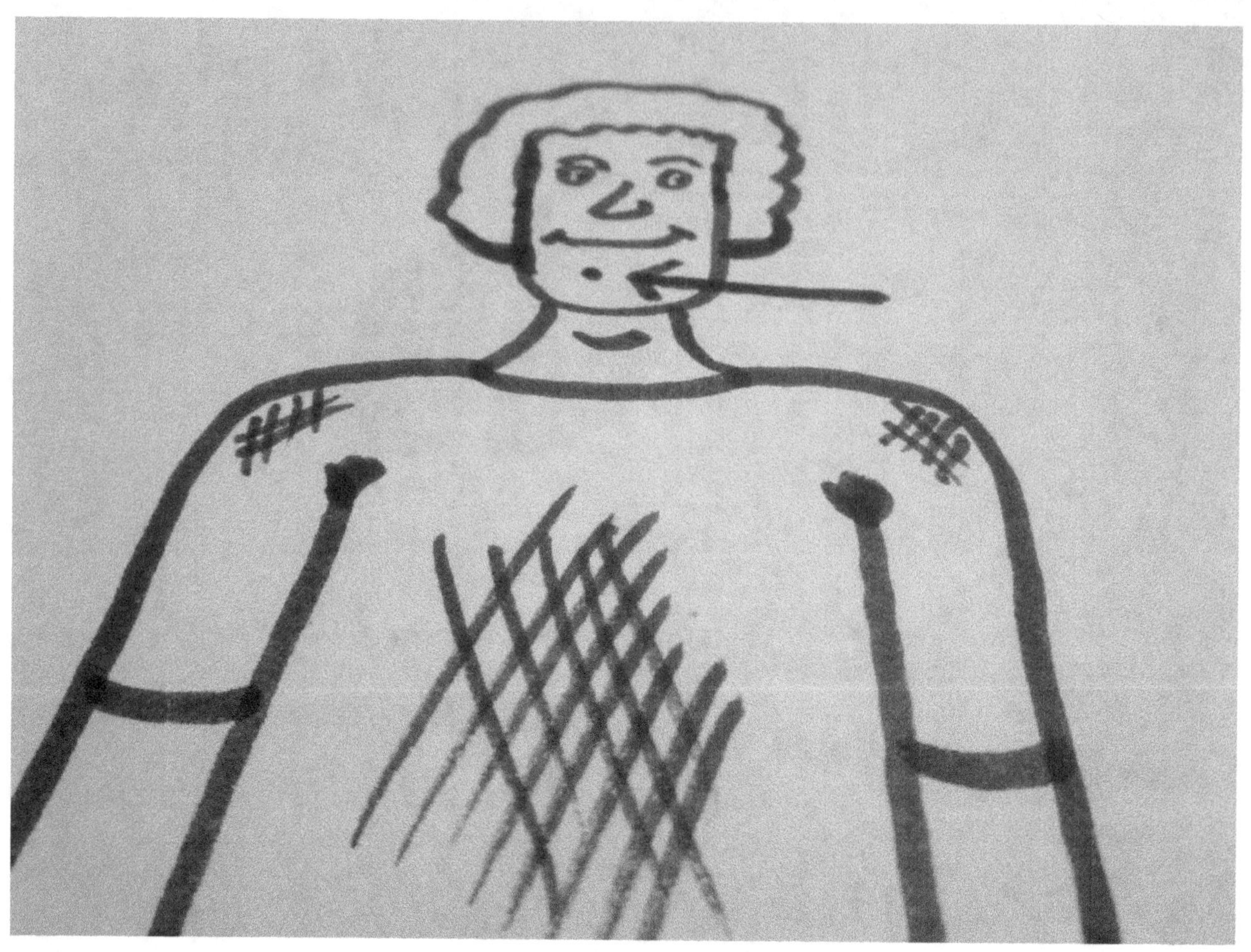

Big Jack Krieg thought that he was one of the smartest fellow's around. But the things that he did, told an entirely different story.

Jim Worley was called Chinly by his family and friends. He had a chin that stuck out very prominently.

Karl Coombs was a big fellow who liked to wear shirts that had statements on them. Very seldom did he wear a shirt that had no writing on it.

Tommy Jakes liked watching Daniel Boone on TV so much, that he ordered a fake Coonskin hat and he wore it almost everywhere he went.

Jerry Denver fell head over heels for the Punk Music scene. He had his hair fixed to look like his music idols. And he started taking guitar lessons in hopes of starting a band someday.

Craig Wakely liked to cut the grass around his home. He liked the smell of the fresh-cut grass and he liked to see the crickets and grasshoppers jumping around as he cut the grass.

Shellie Crayler had a spunky little cat named Cocoa. Cocoa liked to run and play in the beautiful sunshine outdoors. And she liked to eat bacon and tuna fish. And she never turned her nose up to fresh milk in her bowl.

Jim Barton was a pretty-good whistler. He won fifty dollars in a whistling contest when he was in highschool.

Lonnie Becker jumped off the diving board and the judges gave him a high score for his performance in the dive. He went on to college on a diving scholarship and became an attorney for a law firm in Alabama.

Jimmy Blackstone bought his son a metal detector for Christmas. His son used the metal detector to find many interesting things over the next few years. One thing was a gold coin minted in 1847.

Jeremiah Jinks liked to watch his grandfather make pottery on an old pottery wheel. Eventually, his grandfather taught him how to make potter just like himself. And Jeremiah won more than one pottery-making contest.

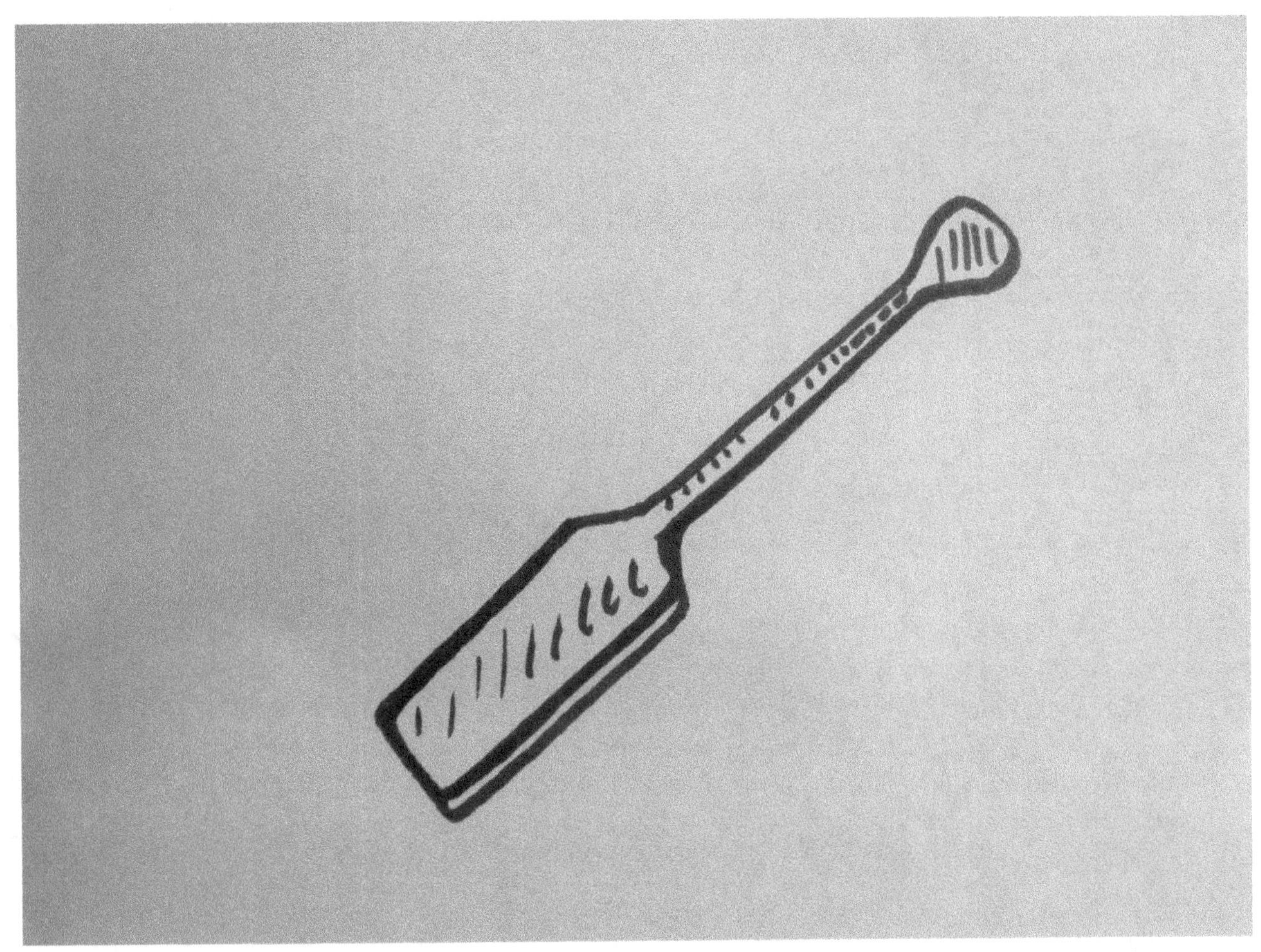

Johnnie Baker made a paddle out of ash wood to use while canoeing down the Blackwater river. His friends told him that he should make paddles to sell, and he began to make more paddles and sold them at a local flea market.

Oliver Flagan baited a hook with a chunk of chicken meat, and then cast the hook out into the bay. In less than thirty seconds, a large fish grabbed the bait and took off with the hook in its mouth. Oliver fought the fish for 30 minutes and then landed the fish with an old dip net. The fish weighed just over 24 pounds.

Ralph Billings would walk around whistling a tune from one of his favorite old songs. He was especially fond of whistling an old Civil War tune that his granddaddy had taught him.

Ted Noonan had on of the meanest old goats that anyone had ever seen. The big billy would put its head down and come charging toward anyone in the yard or anywhere else. It was a bad-mannered goat. A very-bad mannered goat.

Chubby Collins would walk around eating chicken or anything else that he felt like eating. He never worried about how unhealthy a food item was, and he eventually died of a heart attack. He was only 27 years of age. His friends never saw him when he wasn't eating or wasn't fixing to be eating.

Jimmy Hightone had a cat that weighed over twenty pounds. He called the feline Brent. Brent loved to eat tuna fish and mackerel. Jimmy was mighty proud of Brent. He doted on the finicky feline and bragged about it all the time to his family and friends.

Wendie Louise was a flute-playing fool. She was the best flute player that ever attended HallMont High. She eventually won a scholarship to a small college in a town over fifty miles from her home town. She played in the college band and majored in music. Eventually, she joined a professional band and played flute all over the world.

Mack Dean wasn't such a handsome guy, but he had a good personality and that personality helped him win the love of a beautiful young lady named Brianna Gurr. He and Brianna married and had a wonderful life together.

Fuzzie McWinkle had a very fuzzie chin and he was the best guitar picker in Alabama. He was offered a regular gig in a club in Nashville and eventually he got discovered. He traveled all over America and even in Canada playing his own style of music.

Hank Handley sat on a wall and watched the work being done by his employees. And his employees worked even harder than usual while under the close scrutiny of their boss.

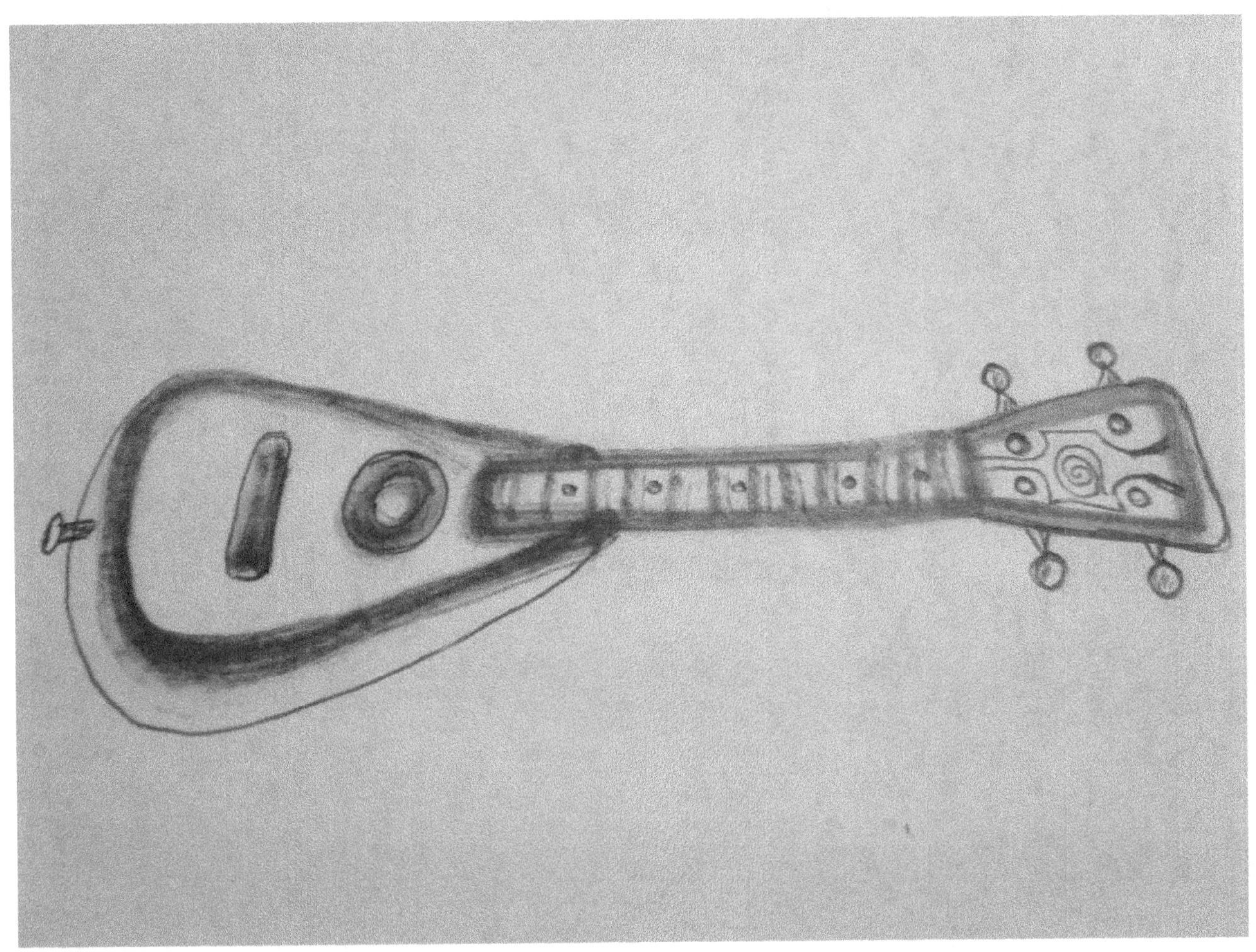

Jimmie Whittie was a ukulele player. He learned to play by taking lessons from a cousin who was a professional musician. Jimmie was a good student and learned to play very well. He later became a professional player himself.

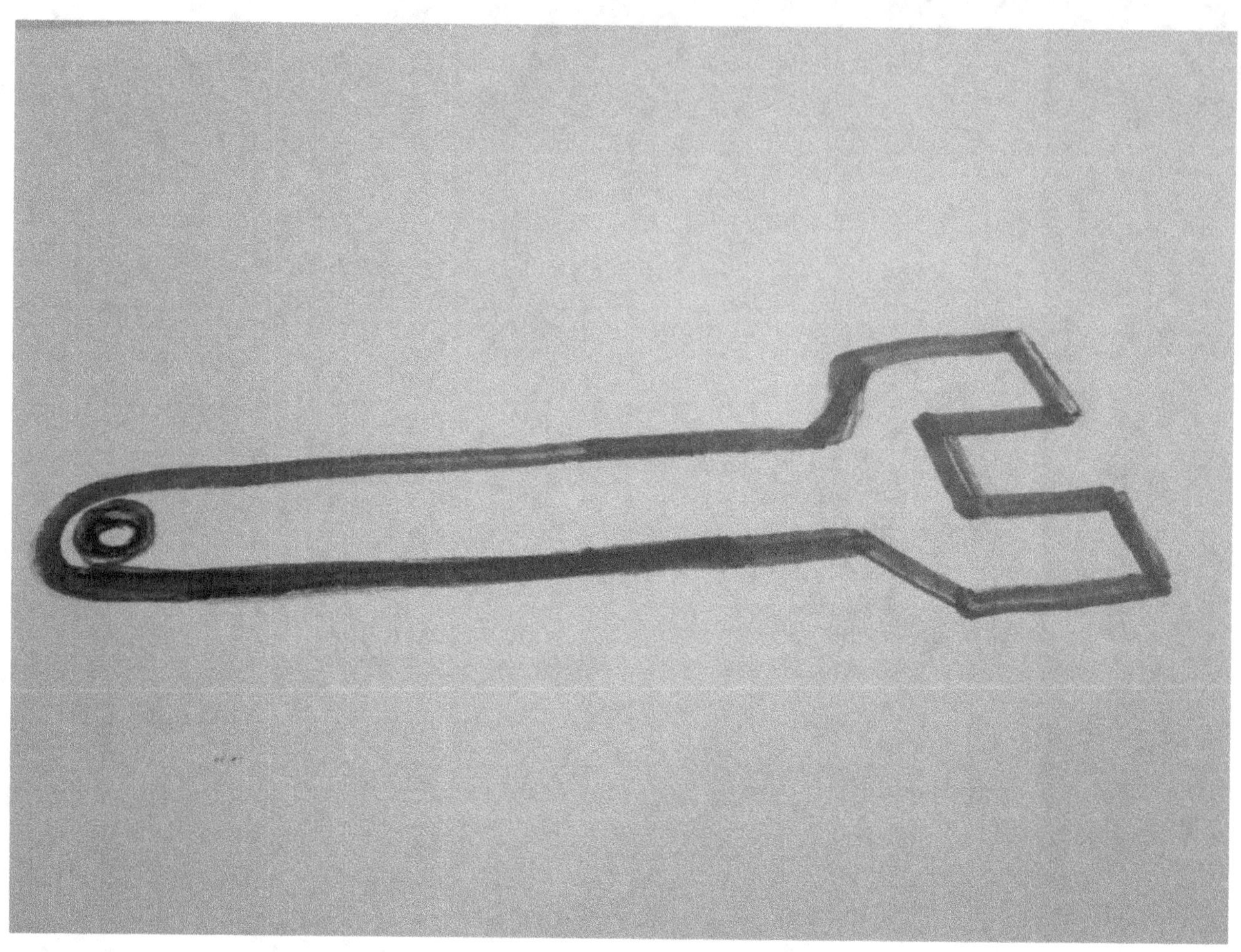

If Tyler Jackson would have brought the proper wrench, he could have fixed his old truck a lot faster. But he had to make do with an old wrench that kept slipping. But, he eventually was able to replace the bolt that had came out of the vehicle.

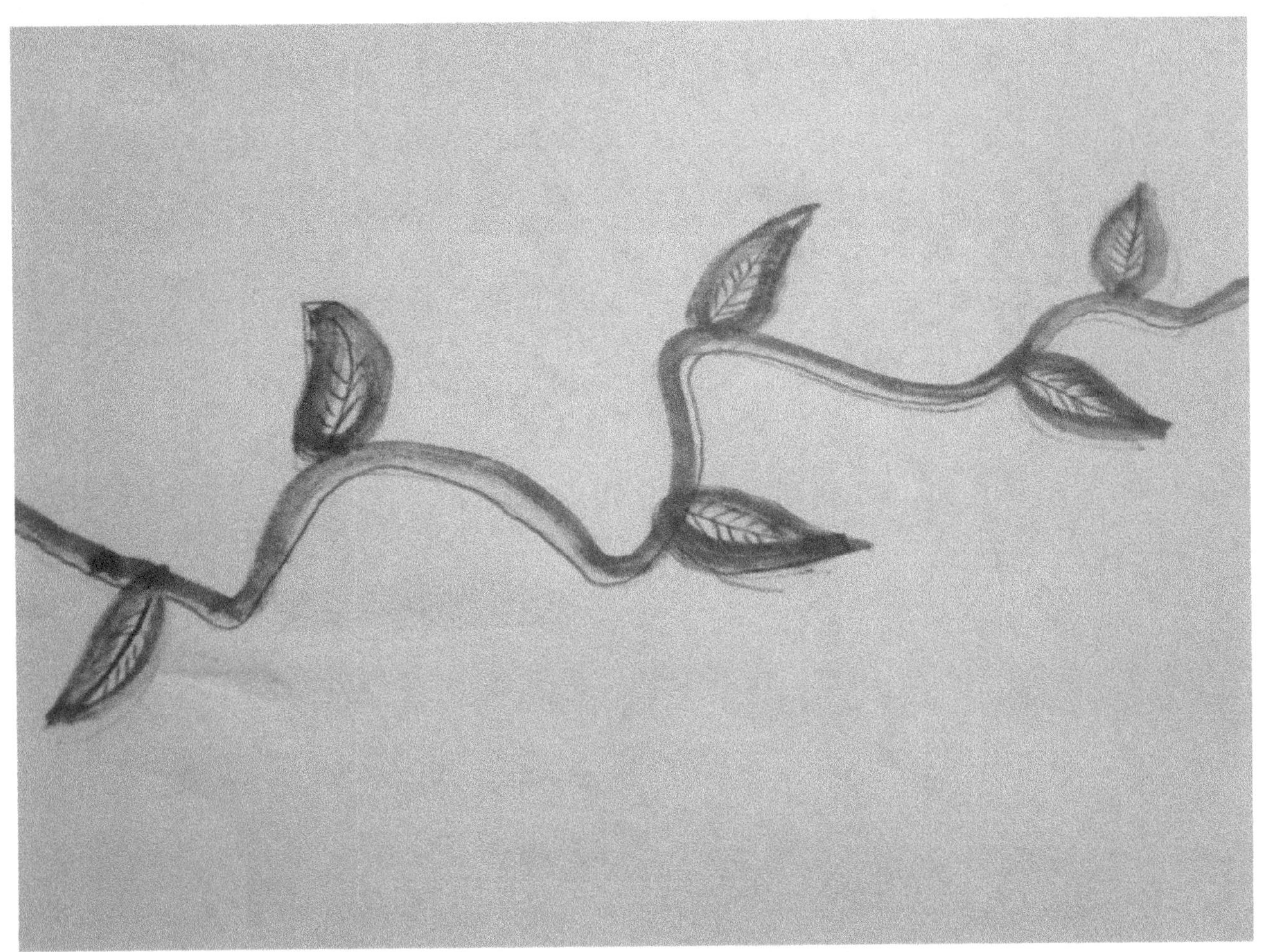

When Tom Watman got to his grandfather's old home place, he noticed that a vine had begun to grow on the side of the shed out back. He wasn't sure what type vine it was, and just in case it was Poison Ivey, he didn't touch it.

Many years earlier, Mr. Winslow Wadsden had planted an acorn. That acorn eventually grew into a large oak tree. Mr. Wadsden was amazed at how the acorn had transformed into a great tree.

For an art project in school, Pam Toler drew a leaf. The leaf was of no particular type, but she received a nice remark from the teacher about the drawing. "Pam, that is a lovely leaf," she said. "You are becoming a fairly-good artist."

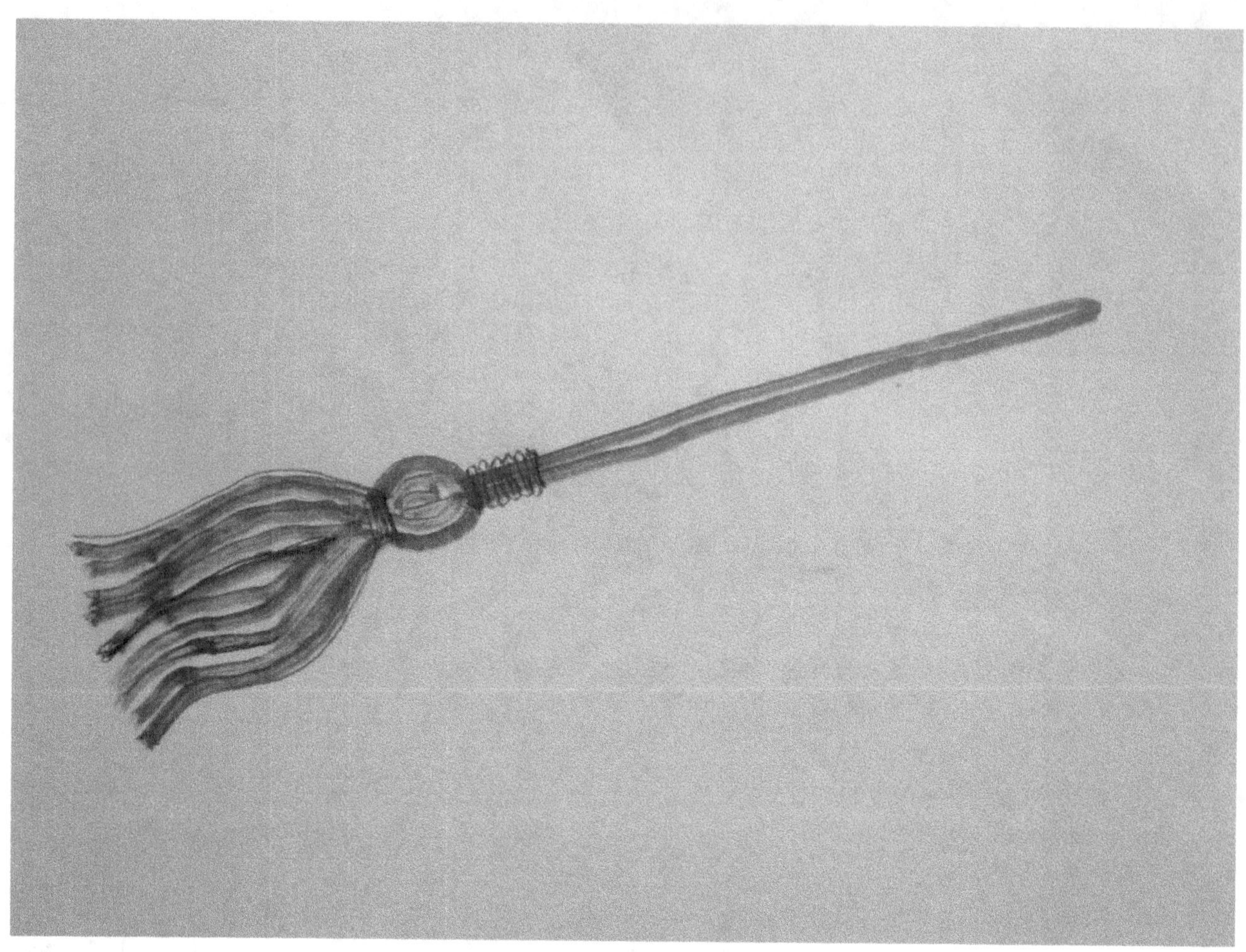

When asked to draw something a witch might use, Maddie Tybdall drew a broom. And her teacher said, "I think a witch would be proud to ride on a broom like that."

Shirley Thomas sewed many pieces of cloth and made a pretty-decent quilt. Someone who visited their home, asked her to enter the quilt into a quilt-making contest, and she won second place in the competition. That encouraged her to make more quilts and to enter into more contests.

Gina Harris didn't believe in ghosts until she encountered one in an old house that she stayed in one night. After that, she was a believer in ghostly matters.

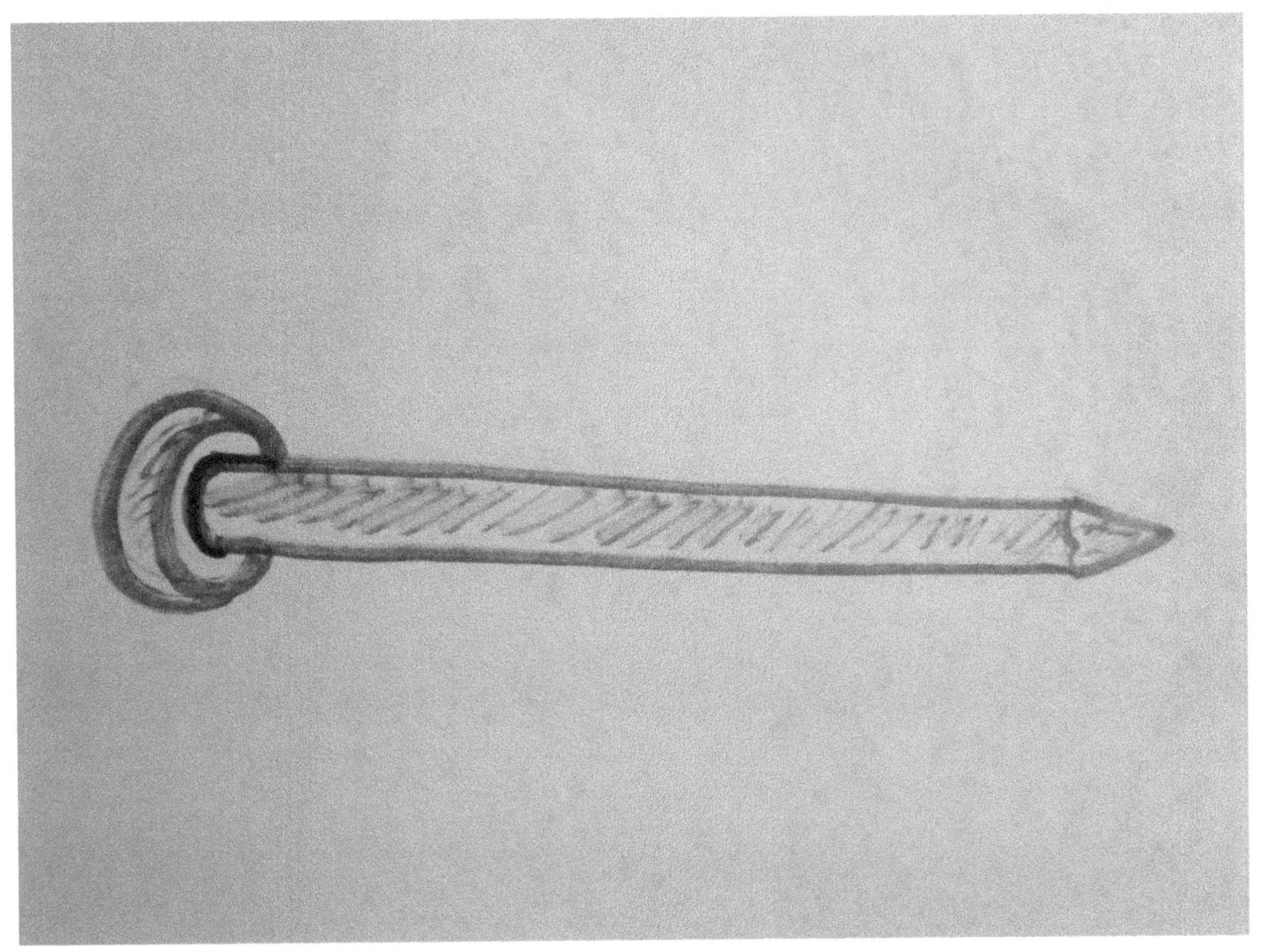

Johnny Pigtree had a flat while coming home from work one evening. He changed the tire, took the tire to a service station, and found out that he had ran over a large nail. After having the tire patched, it was almost as good as new.

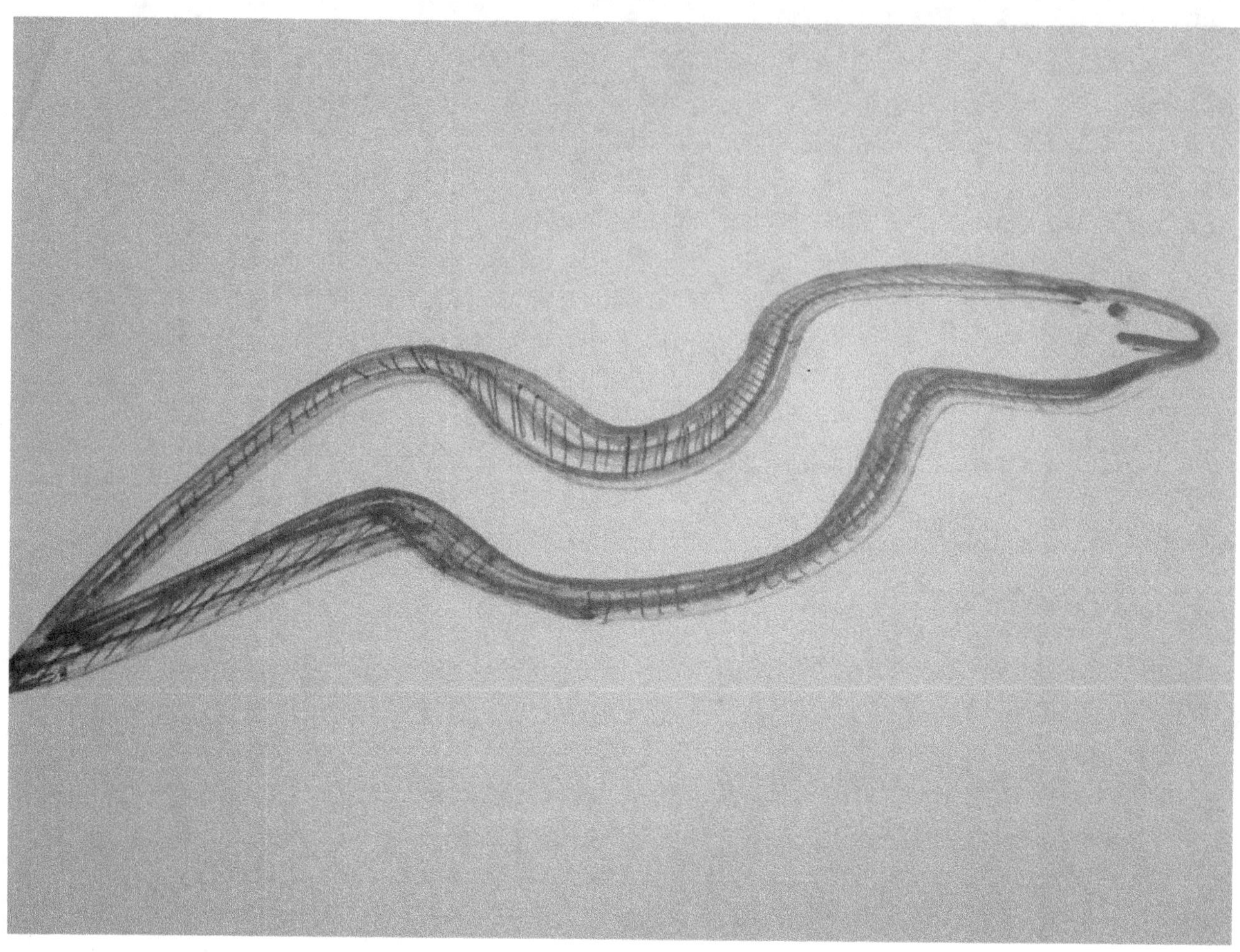

Dennis Rider picked up a board that had been lying on the ground. On the ground where the board had been lying, was a big fat slug. The slug was about three inches long and was about a half inch in diameter.

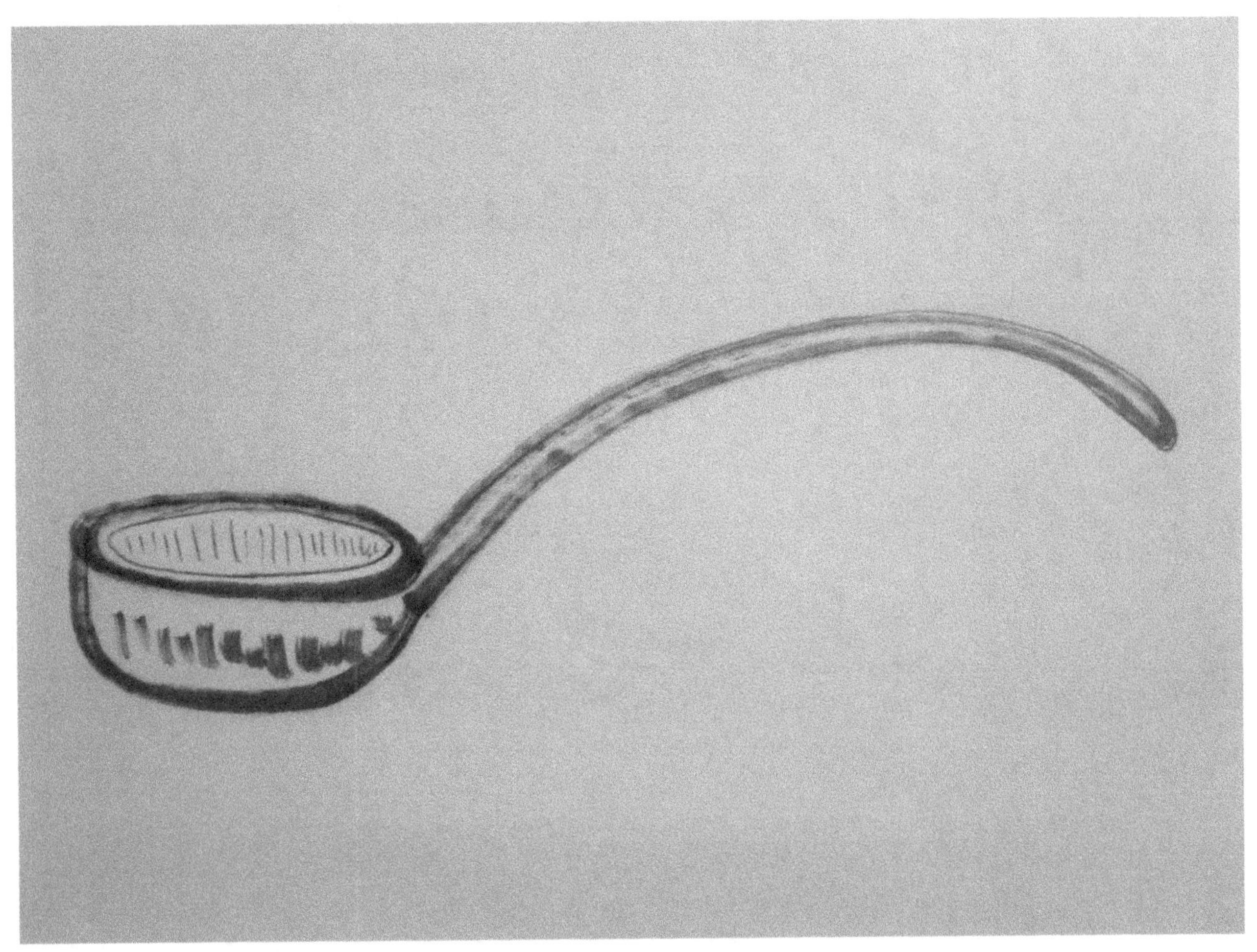

Whenever Paul Creasey looked up at the celestial arrangement called THE BIG DIPPER, he always envisioned that it was an actual dipper like his granddaddy used to have resting near the water bucket on the back porch of his old home.

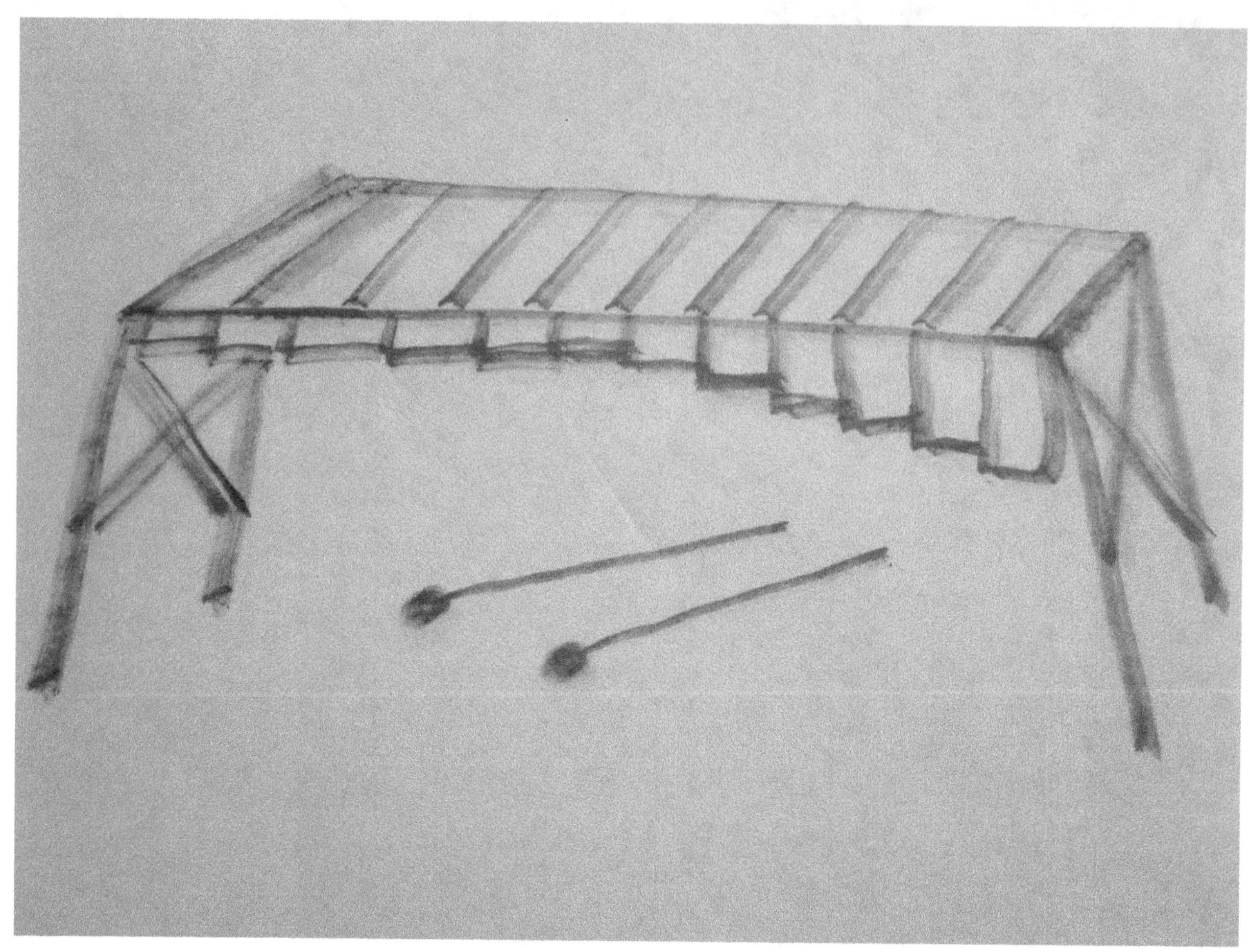

Whenever Brenda Jasper was in high school, the used to play the xylophone. When she graduated from high school, she never played the xylophone again. But she always had fond memories of those days in the school band.

Tim Westfield always wore cloves when he went outside on a cold winter day. He was no fan of cold weather. And he wasn't too keen on having frozen hands.

Chester Klein always thought that he looked really-cool while wearing sun shades. His friends would snicker when he was walking toward them. "Here comes ol' shady" they'd say. And the friends that they said it to would snicker as well. But, they didn't dare let him hear them laughing at him. They knew that he would get angry. Yes, he might get very angry.

Larry Smidt was a deadly shot with a slingshot. He could shoot a bird flying high up in the air as it flew by. No one dared to try to outshoot him, because they knew how accurate he was with his slingshot.

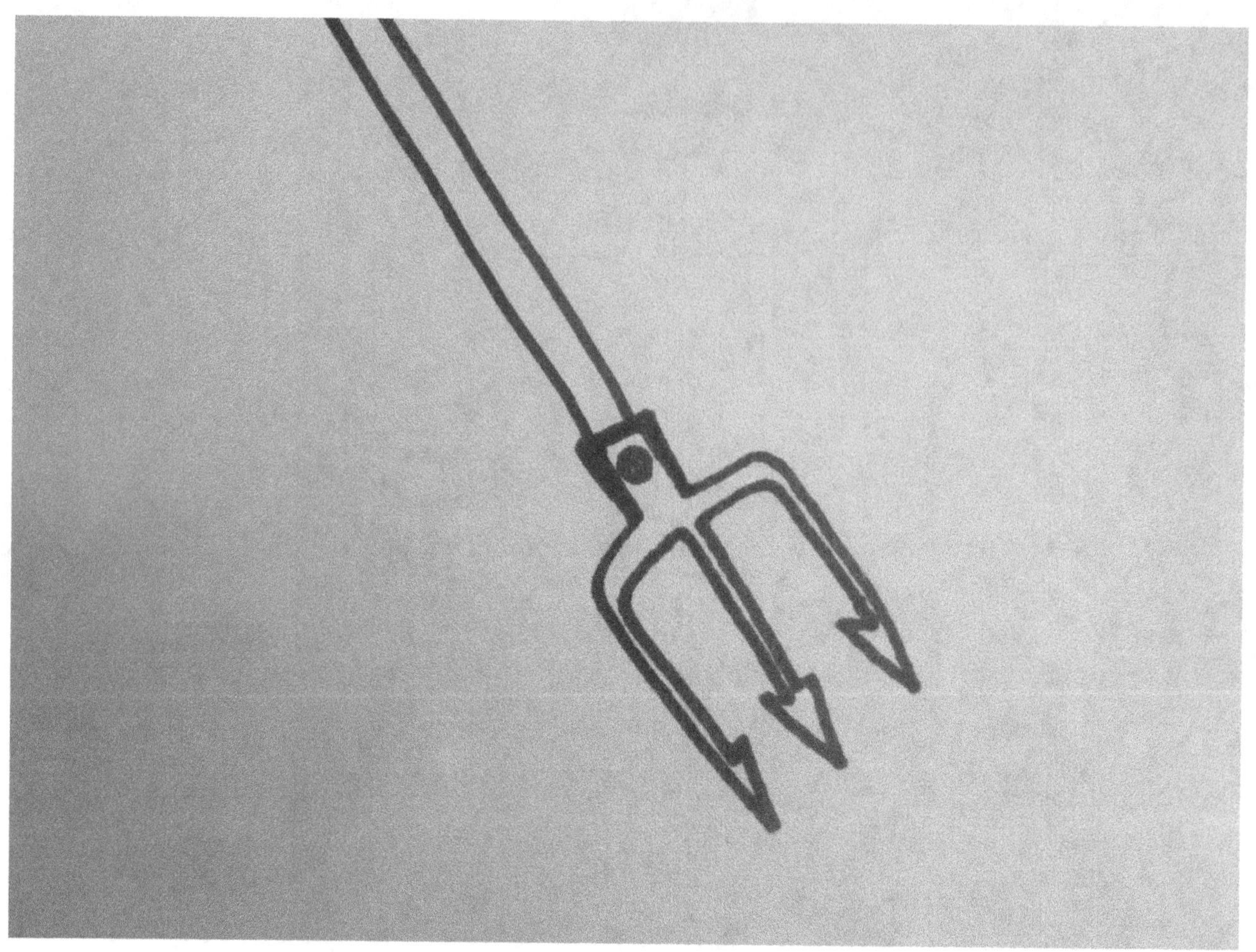

Harley Ballister used to make flounder gigs and sell them to people. He also went floundering and sold the fish to a fish market. He made a lot of extra money doing that. And he would bring a few home and clean them. His wife would cook them and they would have a fine dinner or supper of flounder, hush puppies, and French fries.

Charley Morley liked to make bird houses and sell them down at the local flea market. He liked to talk to the customers about birds and bird houses, etc. And he sold quite a number of his homemade bird houses.

Billy Baxton was a really-tough fellow. Folks said that he was one of the best nunchuck users that they'd ever seen.

Winton Webley was a very accurate archer. He liked using a longbow and he thought of himself as a sort of Robin Hood character. No one argued with him because he was so talented at shooting his bows and arrows.

Waylon Cress liked to ride around in his souped-up car at a high rate of speed. He managed to get several tickets in a couple months, and eventually he had his license taken away and he could be seen riding around in a friend's car, or riding his bicycle.

Benny FigPaw wrote a song that became very popular in the area that he lived in. He was encouraged to move to Nashville, and when he did, he didn't have much luck in the music business and came back home and went to work in his daddy's service station.

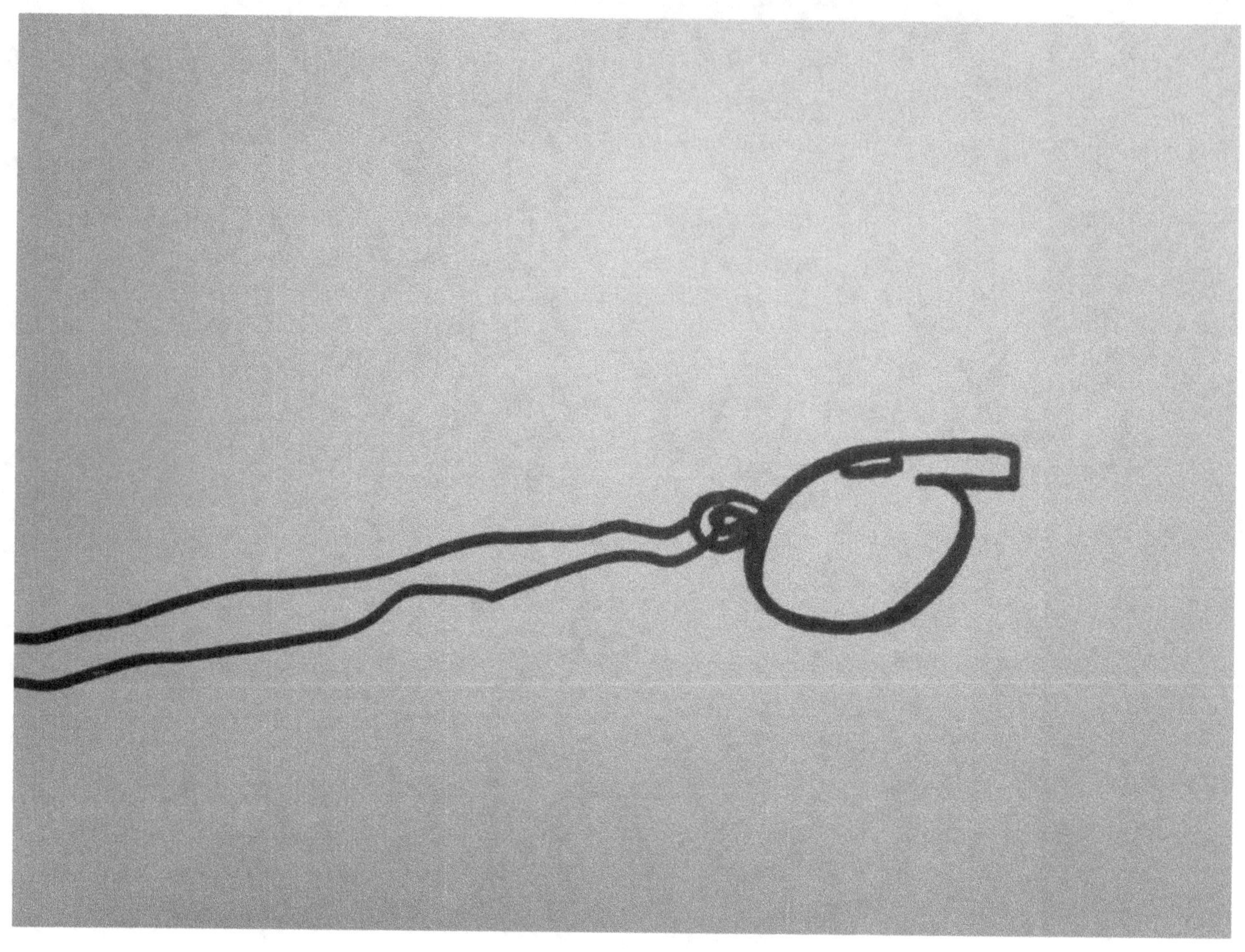

Jimmy Jacks always started off the foot race at the county picnick by blowing an old whistle that his granddaddy had used for many years to start off the foot race at the county picnick. The whistle emitted a really-shrill and loud sound, and the racers would dash like crazy toward the finish line.

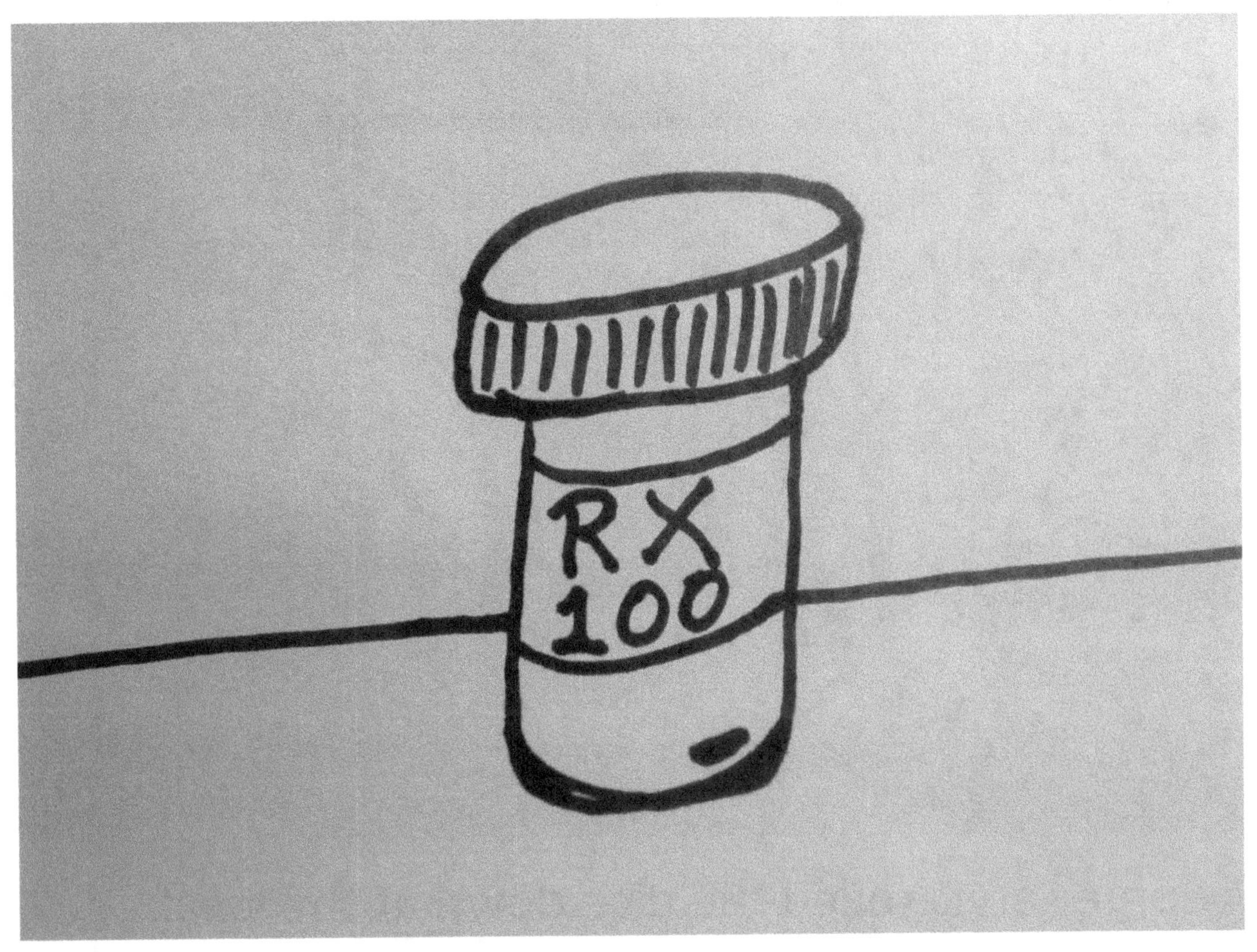

Jillian Jackson wished that she didn't have to take the medication to curb her diabetes problem, but she did. Twice a day. Every day. "It's just the way things have to be," her doctor said. "It's better to be safe. Not sorry."

George Larvis rolled the dice down at the local casino and won seven hundred thousand bucks. He jumped for joy. And he got security to walk him to his car. In a few days, he had quit his job and had started a business selling musical instruments. He would sit around playing guitars and pianos when no customers were in the store.

Harry Henson was a constant smoker. He owned a large pipe collection. He died of lung cancer just before his 34th birthday.

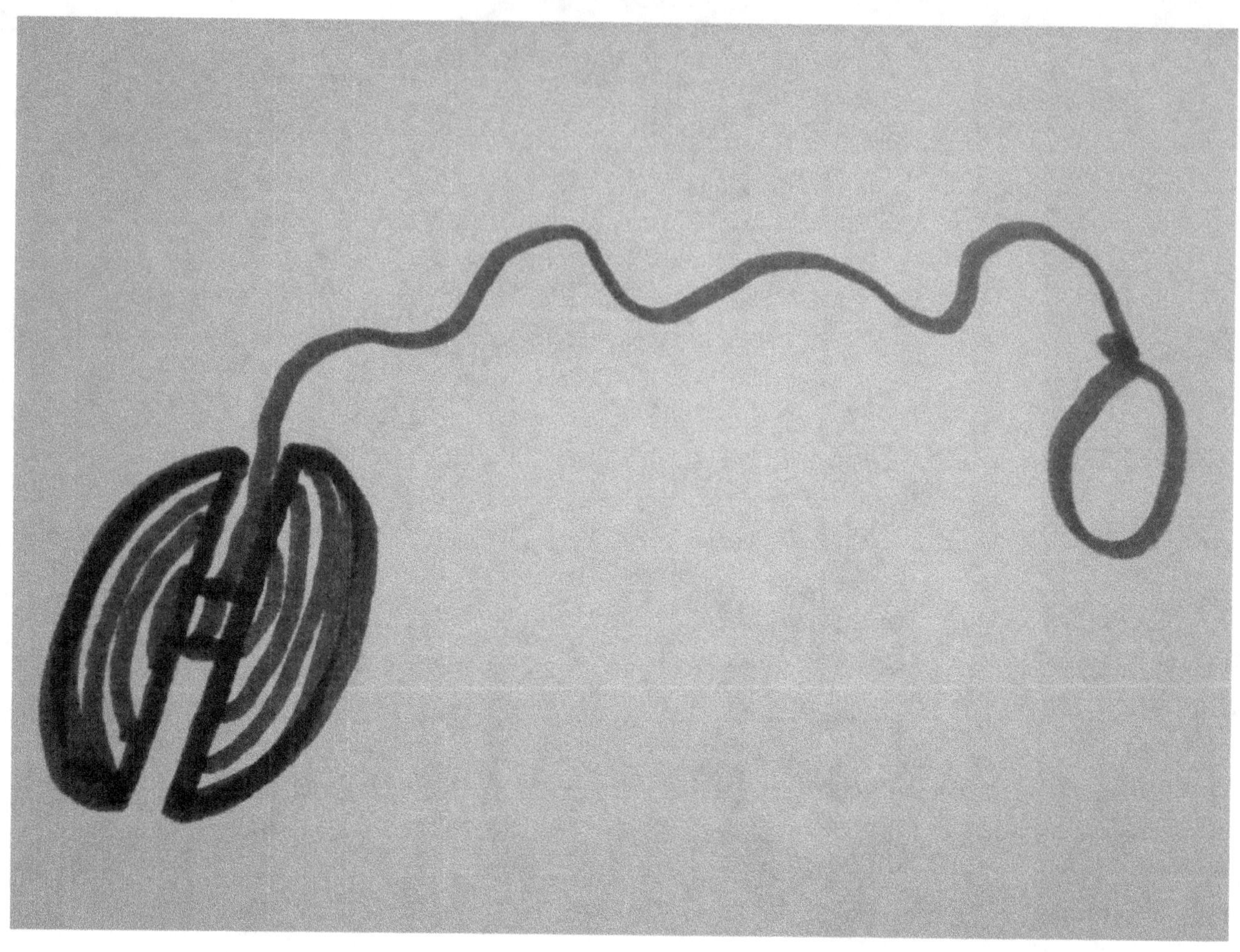

Johnny Bixlee received a Yo-Yo as a gift from his aunt Becky when he was six. He kept that Yo-Yo all the rest of his life. When he passed away, his daughter placed the Yo-Yo in the casket with his lifeless body. And she smiled and said in a quiet voice, "I thought you'd appreciate this, dad."

www.ingramcontent.com/pod-product-compliance
Lightning Source LLC
Chambersburg PA
CBHW080745120726
48001CB00009B/2691